Frank Ronan

Frank Ronan was born in 1963 in Ireland. *The Men Who Loved Evelyn Cotton*, his first novel, won the 1989 *Irish Times*/Aer Lingus Literature Prize. Since then he has published the novels *A Picnic in Eden*, *The Better Angel* and *Dixie Chicken*, as well as a collection of short stories, *Handsome Men Are Slightly Sunburnt*. He has also had work published in *Best Short Stories*, *The Best of Cosmo Fiction* and the *Daily Telegraph*, as well as broadcast on BBC Radio 4.

SCEPTRE

Lovely

FRANK RONAN

SCEPTRE

First published in 1996 by Hodder and Stoughton
A division of Hodder Headline PLC
A Sceptre Paperback

A CIP catalogue record for this book is
available from the British Library

ISBN 0 340 66077 5

Printed and bound in Great Britain by
Cox & Wyman Ltd, Reading, Berkshire

Hodder and Stoughton
A division of Hodder Headline PLC
338 Euston Road
London NW1 3BH

LOVE ∫

The point of departure had been chosen with care. Aaron Gunn, being something of a perfectionist, had waited fourteen years before launching himself on this adventure; had waited until his instinct told him that the moment was right.

The idea of it first came to him at the age of nineteen, while walking across the mountains, by accident, from Neapolis to Leonideon in the Peloponnese. It was the first summer that could be called his own, his head colonised with a muddle of philosophy from a year at university and his backside tanned from the island beaches. His rucksack was stolen in Kissimos, on Crete, leaving him with a passport, a Eurorail ticket and not quite enough money for the ferry to Piraeus. An optimist to the core, he wasted no more than a token five minutes in despair, before reasoning that he had lost nothing of any real value. Unburdened, he hitched a lift on a fishing boat to the nearest point on the mainland.

The road to Leonideon dissolved into a dirt track across the mountains, trafficless. The only person he encountered before Cosmos was a boy with a large flock of goats and sheep who, on seeing such a tall and peculiar person striding along in the dusk, ran screaming into the hills in a primitive terror. The words he shrieked impressed themselves on Aaron's mind. Later when he arrived in Athens, he asked their meaning and was told that the boy had shouted, 'It's the devil! The devil!'

In Cosmos he drank coffee and watched the dawn, elevated by more than the altitude. When he came down, to Leonideon, and saw the cliffs dripping red over the town like a butcher's apron, he felt himself to be a changed and happy person. The idea of travelling was sown.

The plan was to travel without any plan at all; to spend a year wandering through the world in the spirit of his walk across the Greek mountains, baggageless and bookless. To be such a stranger that anyone who encountered him might run into the hills at the sight of him. The only thing to be decided in advance was the moment of leaving. Years passed in waiting for this perfect time. Either there wasn't enough money to spare, or his career was at one of its numerous critical points, or he would be involved with some person or another and the dream would be smothered by an illusion of love.

At the age of thirty-two he realised that he had achieved almost everything he had set his mind on. He was successful, as a writer of cookery books, happy, healthy, well-dressed, well-read, well-spoken, well-mannered and well-thought-of. He had the house he wanted to live in, furnished in the way he liked. His friends were devoted and his family loving but at a reasonable distance. There were two loose ends which remained to be tidied. One of them was the great journey and the other was finding the love of his life. It was logical that he should deal with the first while he was still a single man, before he was to be hit over the head with an inescapable emotion.

Despite having been in love, regularly, he had maintained his romantic faith by a theory of mistaken identity. With every disappointment, betrayal or plain fizzling-out he convinced himself that the real thing was still waiting for him. The perfect lover would have all the qualities which he had found attractive, separately, in each of the mistakes. Thus, every time he got it wrong he comforted himself with the thought that he knew a little more about the identity of the ideal, and was more likely to recognise this being on sight. He could never speak of this belief to anyone else, even though he might have been able to defend it by a twisted sort of Platonism. Love, as far as Aaron Gunn was concerned, was a matter too profound to be discussed with anyone but the beloved.

He gave power of attorney to his agent and the keys of his house to his sister, Susan, so that she could keep an eye on things while he was away. Susan also volunteered to foster his cat, which relieved him of the only conscientious objection he had to being away for so long. With the image of the dawn at Cosmos in mind, he set off in an easterly direction, going by train as much as possible. He carried the absolute minimum: a couple of changes of linen, a toothbrush and a diary. His luggage weighed less than a pound. Anything he bought along the way was posted home. In cold climates he bought extra clothing and in warm climates he discarded it. By December he was in southern India. On New Year's Eve he checked out of the Metropole Hotel in Mysore and boarded the train for Goa. That journey, of twenty-four hours in a second-class sleeper, was particularly good. The train crossed the hills at not much more than walking pace and, in that meditative progress, he thought he had found the object of his travelling.

His first impression of Goa was that he would not be tempted to stay there long. His diary entry for New Year's Day was a three-page condemnation of the tourist industry. The entry for the second of January, however, was the shortest so far. It read, 'Baga. Met someone whose name is Lovely.'

The party should have been held the night before. The jungle was painted and the speakers stacked at the edge of the paddy. Chai ladies had carpeted the surrounding fields with their matting. The acid punch was brewed and the police had been given their baksheesh, or so everyone thought. But that was the year that the Goan Press decided to become more than usually hysterical with bourgeois indignation. It was time, the editor decreed, to put a stop to hippies and drug fiends, who corrupted the unsullied minds of Indian Youth and gave the state a bad reputation. That the more acceptable kind of tourists, with their golf courses and swimming pools, were wrecking the agricultural economy, was not a point which the editor, whose friends were hoteliers rather than farm labourers, was likely to raise. The result of the outburst was that the police who, by and large, had paid heavy bribes for Goan postings so that they could become rich by harrassing the hippies and drug fiends, took this unprecedented spate of indignation as their cue to demand even more money from the party organisers. So a thousand ravers spent the night sitting on the chai ladies' mats, waiting for the music to begin, while acrimonious negotiations were being conducted elsewhere.

Some went home and some took their drugs anyway

and wandered down to the beach where they stared, open-mouthed, at the stars. Some had taken so many drugs that they remained pinned to the paddy all night and were able to imagine the music. A deal was struck between the police and the organisers at noon on New Year's Day, and the party became, effectively, a two-day event, and the best party that anyone who had not lost the faculty of memory could remember.

Nick and Cathy were among those who stayed for the duration. That was the party at which they found a little bag of goodies which some dealer must have dropped. They experimented recklessly with the contents, dragging those thirty-six hours out into a lifetime of holiday. Because of the disarrangement and confusion of time they couldn't say exactly when it was that they first noticed the tall man, but it must have been during the second night. He was dancing near the speakers, like an otter, more cadence than rhythm, seeming incongruous with his height, and a precision to him among the sliding ravers in their cloven footwear. Nick and Cathy were themselves trying to dance, but were so far gone that they could only clutch at each other in fits of unwarranted laughter. They lost the plot just after that, and the next thing they could remember was coming away from the dancers and dropping, cross-legged, onto the matting of their chai lady. While Cathy closed her eyes, as a way of retreating into a world she could control more easily, Nick focussed on a raw corrugation of muscle that still twitched in his shoulder, keeping time with the sinuous high hat, which seemed to come separately from the rest of the music, threading through the mango trees. He was devastatingly amused. It was during that distraction that the light changed; night ended and the morning began.

It was while he was sitting like that, grinning like an idiot as he grappled with the last hours of the party, that Aaron first saw him, and began to be fascinated.

So many party rumours had been washing over Baga on New Year's Day, and so many strangers had asked Aaron whether he had been to the party and whether he was going, and whether he knew what the truth was, that he had decided, in the cause of disinterested scholarship, to go and see what the fuss was about. Once there, he had swallowed a tab of something mild and dancy and enjoyed the spectacle while he waited for it to kick in.

Though he danced and exchanged mindless smiles with other dancers and gave himself all the evidence that he was having a good time, he became conscious of his isolation. He began to think of the end of his travels, when he would return home, alone, to the perfect universe he had created for himself. He had to remind himself that his life was a happy one, was the life he had chosen; but the acid in his brain would not allow the usual arguments for self-satisfaction. That word, *alone*, kept repeating in his mind. Like someone who has failed his driving test and is watching all the cars on a busy road, wondering what is wrong with him that he cannot accomplish such a simple and everyday skill, he saw couples everywhere he looked and felt himself to be a failure. It occurred to him that he was already in love, and that he had been in love all his life, but without finding the object of his love. If he didn't find it soon he might become a selfish old bachelor, too fussy about his petty and ordered life to allow another to infringe upon it.

Having thought all this, in the syncopated meter of dancing, and having reached what had the semblance of a decision, he had been overtaken by a calmness and walked away from the music. That was when he saw Cathy and Nick.

The sky was paling indigo and the light at ground level was intense and greenish from the lamps of the chai ladies. Nick was minding his own business, tripping his tits off and smiling the width of an ache, with Cathy beside him in a lesser stupor. On seeing them, the first thing Aaron thought was that this couple were the perfect illustration of what he had just been wanting, that they had some knowledge which was denied to him. He had never seen a creature so evidently, unashamedly and completely happy as Nick. It was not Nick that first attracted him, but Nick's happiness. From the way they sat together, it could be assumed that Nick and Cathy were lovers; that Nick was not available. Aaron watched the smiling man and something changed; something was signified. He could not tell what or how, but he knew that he would have to find out; that he would have to find a way of talking to this person. He had a feeling that his failure was about to be overturned.

The chai lady nearest to him was holding out a glass of coffee and asking, in an insistent voice, whether he wanted it. He folded his legs beneath him and took the glass. Through the dawn and the morning he watched the pair, making guesses as to who they were and what their relationship was. They seemed to know everyone who passed or, if they didn't, to be ready to know anyone. Aaron couldn't make out anything they said, but he could read their gestures. From the way that one of them would point out a good-looking man to the other, and the smutty look they would exchange in consequence, it soon became obvious that they were no more than friends. By this time Aaron was too involved in romantic fantasy to notice that this realisation had overturned the original motivation for his interest in them. It took a very small leap of the imagination for Aaron to think that he was falling in love.

Towards the end of the party the midday sun seemed devastating. There had been stretches of time when the morning had given the impression of running on for eternity. The dawn had been diverting, followed by the appearance of thick clouds of dust between the dancers and the light. Palm trees changed from kitsch silhouettes to vegetation. Then a trick of the drug would scatter time and hours would be lost to memory, as though the noon was grafted onto the night and nothing at all had happened in between, and all the debris on the paddy fields had come from nowhere.

As the hottest part of the day began and the light became searing on his dilated pupils, Nick began to worry. He had reached the stage where it seemed that the trip would never end, trapping him forever in this condition of helplessness. He wondered if he had overdone it this time. Goa was stuffed with acid casualties, those who had taken one trip too many and never come back. He tried to think of normality, and to remember how his mind had functioned before the party. The distance covered in the previous thirty hours seemed so preposterous that he laughed out loud. Then the question of whether he had permanently lost his mind was overtaken by a ringing in his teeth, and nothing mattered but a desperate search for chewing gum.

As Aaron watched and fell in love, every detail became clear in the harshness of the light. Nick, unconscious that anyone was taking so much notice, had his arms crossed, stroking his cleavage as though he were cold, his jaw working at a rhythmic speed and his gaping pupils focussing on one point and another in logicless succession. If it had been in his power to choose a state in which to be described, or seen, for the first time, almost any other condition might have been preferable. Sweat had run and dried on him, holding a fresco of red dust over his skin and clothing. Beneath these layers was the frame of a man who had been skinny in his youth, gone to the gym in his twenties, and suffered the creeping tide of flesh that had spread from his middle in the four years since he had turned thirty. His hair would have been a sort of blond colour had it not been cut down to an eighth of an inch to mitigate a receding line, his eyebrows were white and his lashes invisible. Supporting all these was a face of a standard handsomeness, of the kind that looks good in photographs and is otherwise dependent on the expression it bears. Smiling, as it was now, it was undeniably attractive. A large hand, holding a joint, was positioned delicately, as if that joint had an irreplaceable significance. Without it, the prospect of walking two hundred yards of jungle path to find a rickshaw was unthinkable.

The remains of the party were thinning by the minute. Soon there would be no music and it was important to get away before then. It was awful to leave a dead party, and not hear the thump of the speakers ebb as you got further away, never fading completely because your overworking imagination would dub sound into the silence, and your bones would twitch as though it were sound you had in your bloodstream and not acid.

Nick glanced at the spliff between his fingers, expelled all the air that was in him, and found himself standing on his feet, wishing that he had someone to talk to.

'Are we going then?'

Cathy's voice had come from somewhere near his knees. He remembered, first, that she had been there all the time and, second, that it was she who had skinned up and handed him the joint.

He began to laugh, not because it was hilarious to have momentarily forgotten Cathy's existence, but as a result of another thing that was happening at the same time. For the previous ten minutes he'd been staring at a television set, amazed that there could be such a thing in the middle of the jungle. Then the television began to move towards him, which was even more astonishing. He was still trying to work out what programme was being shown when he realised that he had, in fact, been watching the design on a tall man's T-shirt.

'I've lost it, sweetie,' he said. 'I'm so off my face that I thought that man was a telly.'

Cathy looked in Aaron's direction while Nick helped her to her feet.

'Babysweets,' he said.

She nailed him with a look so cynical that he wondered whether she had taken any drugs at all. 'Stop that,' she growled. 'Any more slush like that and I'm going to bed with a valium when we get home. You can come down on your own for the day.'

While Nick tended to get sentimental on drugs Cathy remained so much herself that you wondered why she bothered. She knew that he was afraid of coming down and that he needed to be accompanied back to reality. The threat of her taking valium could prevent him from uttering sickening endearments for several minutes at a time. In practice though, they had known each other for so many years, and been on so many trips together, that there was no question of them not chilling out together.

Cathy was a woman whose proportions were all squares and cubes, like a diagram from one of those textbooks on how to draw the human figure. Her nose and her chin were boxes and her shoulders formed a straight line, as if they had been shaped with pegs and string. When she turned to look at you she swivelled like a Rubick's Puzzle. Over the years, at various times, she and Nick had lived together and worked together and taken holidays together and seen each other through a frightening accumulation of disastrous relationships. If they had never had a serious fight it was owing, largely, to her fierceness. He would never have dared argue with her on a vital issue. She was the sort of person who liked or hated you on sight, and if you were liked you were made to stay liked. If you were hated you might as well shoot yourself in the head and call it an economy measure.

Nick asked, 'Shouldn't we be looking for Fergus and Andrew?' He could remember that they had all arrived at the same time.

'Fuckwit,' she said. 'They went home at three this morning. You spent an hour saying goodbye to them.'

'I forgot. Sorry. Don't be cross, it isn't my fault.' Then, in an ironic tone intended, but failing, to disguise the seriousness of his question, he said, 'But you love me really, don't you?'

'No,' she said, gathering up their possessions from the mats with a disturbing efficiency. 'Only when you're not so bloody irritating. And that's hardly ever.'

He had the feeling that they had been standing for a long time, as though they had forgotten the reason for getting to their feet. Nick muttered something about vestibule paralysis, but Cathy either failed to understand or thought the expression unremarkable, and then Nick failed to see its relevance himself. Their eyes wandered the paddies, resting on each of the remaining chai ladies and their entourages of half-dressed and tattooed Europeans. There were jugglers here and there, in silly hats, but they were to be ignored, because there was something immodest about them and the way they practised their trivial craft so publicly. They claimed it was a form of meditation, but it looked more like showing-off.

Nick began to say goodbye to Anya, the chai lady they came back to at every party. She sat, placid and competent, amidst her web of kettles and basins of water, guarding the basket which contained her customers' coats and bags, behind the plates of cakes and biscuits that no one, however hungry, would buy and which were alleged to be years old, kept in a rusty tin through the rainy season.

In an unlikely moment of clarity, Nick asked Cathy if they had paid yet.

'Ages ago.' Cathy was counting the bracelets on her wrist before setting off.

'Did we give her loads?'

'Masses. Tons. A hundred rupees more than she asked for.'

They liked to be extravagant with Anya. A hundred rupees might not seem like a lot but it would have been a fortune to her. Nick sometimes thought that she should show more gratitude, but she'd only smile slightly at the corner of her mouth. That, apparently, was the way things were done in India. Someone who'd been reading a guidebook had told someone else Nick knew that there was no word in Hindi for 'thank you'. Cathy said that Anya, who was an astute businesswoman in other respects, might have done a bit more research into Western requirements, good manners costing nothing and all that.

As far as Anya was concerned, the finer feelings of her jelly-brained clients were the least of her worries. She was saving for a dowry. Having her sights set on the best sort of husband that money could buy, she had turned down three suitors already. She was gambling on a sliding scale of gold and fecundity and would go on selling oversweetened coffee to narco-tourists until the last possible moment of her eligibility, when she would pass her kettles and her cream horns on, to the next of her unmarried sisters. Privately, she had little sympathy for young people who would travel halfway round the world to spend their nights staring into blank space.

They seemed to be on the verge of moving. 'Next time, no other lady,' Anya warned, by way of leavetaking. At the same time she was scanning the field for potential new clients, calling out to them. There were fewer people now, and most of the other chai ladies were packing up to go home. Anya was usually the last to leave. When the right man came along she wanted to have the price of him in her choli.

Nick followed close behind Cathy and held her fingers loosely, as though he were in danger of losing her. He had a suspicion that he might be on the verge of thinking something important, but then he shook his head and tripped a little instead, watching a boy who was dancing alone on a mound behind the speakers. His arms were writhing, describing letters against the sky, or so it seemed, but Nick was never a great one for reading.

Cathy said, without turning or looking at him, 'So where was Mr Right, then?'

He couldn't tell, from the back of her head, whether she was joking or not.

'Cathy?' he said. 'Are you happy?'

She made a noise like a horse whose face is half buried in feed.

He heard himself telling her that he was happy. He was glad to hear himself say that.

'Cathy?' he added. 'Don't take valium when we get back, please. I'm going to need you. You know what it's like when you come down and have to face all that stuff littered around in your brain.'

'I am blessed,' she said, 'with a tidy mind.'

'And if we get desperate we could have a bhang lassi, or if we get the munchies we could go to the Two Sisters' for muesli, and I'll rub your back if you like.'

'You are babbling now.'

He pulled on her hand. 'Can we stop? I'm just having a bit of a moment.'

He bent his head to her and she put her arms about his waist. 'Your hair,' she said, 'looks red. It must be the dust.'

'So long as I'm not turning ginger.'

'No,' she said. 'Can you walk now?' She stood back a little and considered his legs as if she had doubts about their design.

Looking down it, the fifty yards of jungle path that remained seemed an impossible distance. The roar of motorbikes was louder now than the music. There was a bullock nearby, with painted horns, grazing on cigarette butts and roaches. Fear of the animal gave Nick the courage he needed to go on.

'Do you think,' he asked, 'that I am the only European in Goa without a tattoo?'

'Shall we just concentrate on walking?'

A tall man brushed past them as she spoke. Nick saw the back of his head.

At the end of the path there was only one auto-rickshaw left among the rows of hundreds of motorbikes, and the tall man was already standing beside that, in conversation with the driver. That was when Nick became conscious of the man's face for the first time. He was the one whose T-shirt had been mistaken for a television; the one who had been dancing alone in the night. Apart from that, there was something strongly familiar about him, in the angle of his shoulder and the incline of his head, as though he were someone whom Nick had known a long time before, whose appearance had changed but whose essence had remained.

Aaron turned and looked at Nick directly. It may have been narcotic delusion, but he was under the impression that Aaron had been aware of his presence before turning. Caught in that line of vision, Nick stopped breathing, only realising that he had done so when he found himself gasping for air.

He seemed unforgivably tall, and he had a way of leaning back from his height as though he needed to view the world from even further away. His face was long and his eyes were long and he looked as though he had come from another dimension, to pass judgment. He made Nick feel naked and ashamed, made him think that here was a man he would never be able to hide anything from. Nick thought him beautiful – the most attractive man he had ever come across – but his looks were so unusual that he could just as easily have called him ugly. His mouth made you think of the word orifice.

His clothes were a little too clean for someone who had spent the night at a party. Nick assumed that he was one of those creatures who turn up at the edge of the dancefloor in the morning, shaven and pure and not there to dance but for the sake of superciliousness. Yet he knew, at the same time, that he had felt the presence of this man the whole night. There's no accounting for the ideas that drugs will put in your mind.

Nick had his back to a wall, for which he was grateful, and he leaned against it. He had a sensation that he was being pushed into the stone by the way the man was looking at him. He closed his eyes as a method of evasion, and concerned himself with the problem of whether or not he should spit out the gum, which had turned to wet blanket but was, as far as he knew, the last piece. Under the darkness of his eyelids he began to trip in colours, smiling at the sight and worried, at the same time, that the man by the rickshaw might think the smile was for him.

Cathy was speaking, but he lost several seconds before working out that he would have to open his eyes to see who it was she was talking to.

Afterwards, he could only remember that he had said to her, 'Sorry sweetie, but I've lost it completely.' At the time it seemed important to supply her with that information, as if she couldn't have guessed it for herself.

The ride home might have been dreamt. He could not, in retrospect, distinguish what had happened from what he had imagined. He knew that they took a track across a field, bouncing and speeding, and that he was slumped and wedged between Cathy and the strange man. Now and then he could open his eyes and focus on the driver's rear-view mirror and see the eyes of Aaron Gunn. They were pale brown, with a rim of violet on the circumferences of the pupils, and they appeared to be always fixed on Nick. He heard conversation, but he could make no sound himself. He may have imagined the moment when he glanced into the man's lap and saw the outline of an erection in the green cotton.

Nick was mistaken in thinking that Aaron had an erection, but it was a mistake easily made, since Aaron had a dick which was not only of respectable proportions, but also had a tendency towards the perpendicular at its most passive moments. Nick was right, on the other hand, to think that there was something familiar about the man. Aaron had occasionally appeared on daytime television, in the cookery slots. Neither was he mistaken when he thought that Aaron was staring at him in the rear-view mirror throughout the ride from Chapora to Baga. Aaron was fascinated by the fact that Nick, whether he was sleeping or not, never quit smiling the whole journey.

The smile was, in part, because Nick had decided to fall in love with the tall man. For the moment, this was no more than a fantasy. He had taken enough drugs in his time to know that he was in no position to make life-altering judgments. Too often, he'd gone home with the most beautiful man in the club, only to discover a changeling beside him in bed next morning. Nevertheless, he liked the idea of love at first sight, and so was not averse to an instant crush on a strange man met in exotic circumstances. Later, if his bluff was called and the stranger declared himself to be the man of Nick's dreams, the fantasy could easily be exaggerated to fill the requirements of instant, fated passion.

There would be no need to mention the fact that his heart used to stop in the same way every time he saw a handsome man on the top deck of a bus. That is the sort of unnecessary detail which spoils the story. The beloved, Nick knew, would need to feel unique in some respect.

Nick remembered little of this afterwards, apart from a vague sense of attraction. He had to piece it together from what he was told by the other two before he could give a convincing account of it himself.

Sometime between leaving Anya and arriving at the rickshaw, Cathy realised the extent to which he had lost it. She was one of those people who become responsible and efficient on acid. She knew that no matter how fried and refried her brain might be she could still concentrate on one thing and get it done. Her task, she decided, was to get Nick back to the Gregory Garden as quickly as possible. There was only one rickshaw and the fact that it was already spoken for was not a circumstance to thwart her.

Fortunately for Aaron he was also staying in Baga, just down the road from the other two, which made it logical to share the rickshaw, and saved Cathy from using the full power of her elbows to secure her interests. Afterwards, he maintained that had they been going in opposite directions he would have lied about his destination rather than let Nick out of his sight. This would also have fitted neatly into his theory about travelling by serendipity.

Cathy said that she had arranged the seating so that Nick came between her and Aaron because she was instinctively revolted by him. Aaron said that he had arranged the seating so that he could put his arm across Nick's shoulders without it seeming contrived. They both said that Nick was semi-conscious by that time, making incoherent remarks about jungle television.

According to her, Aaron did most of the talking: speaking fluently on trivial subjects; monopolising the conversation as if he had no doubt but that he was the most interesting and entertaining person on the sub-continent. She said that he told her so much about himself that she began to wonder what his motives could be. If she couldn't remember any of it afterwards she blamed the drugs and her lack of interest. He said that he was silent for most of the journey, feeling the length of Nick's thigh alongside his own. All of the accounts were, in essence, true.

As they drew near Baga, Cathy's instinct persuaded her that the interloper should be dropped off first, so that he wouldn't know where they were staying.

'We could all have a drink sometime,' he said, as he stood in the road outside his hotel, which was one of those places with a swimming pool, a bar-b-que buffet and lavatories you could sit on.

'Perfect,' she muttered, unsmiling and unforthcoming, and she drew back into the gloom of the rickshaw, setting her sunglasses more squarely on her face.

He asked her where they were staying and she didn't bother to reply. The rickshaw sputtered away from him and she pulled the flopping Nick in close to her, and ran her finger near the hairline down the right-hand side of his forehead.

'Jammy bugger,' she said.

'What?' He discovered that he could speak if he kept his eyes closed.

'You always manage to be out of it when the worst things happen. You missed a right one there.'

Nick made a noise that was meaningless even to himself, and they crossed Baga Bridge, with his head lolling about like an overbred dahlia.

At the northern end of Baga beach, a river runs out into the sand. At low tide it can be crossed on foot, if you hitch your lungi about your waist. Otherwise there is the Baga Bridge, which is a kind of architectural wonder: a concrete tunnel elevated six feet higher than the road it was built to serve. Rickshaw drivers are prepared to charge at it full tilt, but a taxi will make a massive detour rather than risk the chassis; cyclists are forced to dismount and carry their machines into the gloom of the interior. The stones on either side are marked with the blood of motorcyclists.

The Gregory Garden, where Nick and Cathy were staying, was on the inconvenient and quieter side of this river, beneath the hill of rock and scrub and cashew plantation which divided Baga from Anjuna below the monastery from which nuns in peach-coloured saris emerged at sunset to meditate on the cliffs. It was a large, square, Goan house at the centre of a garden within sight of the sea, among the small houses and wells of a settlement that was no longer quite a village. People came to the Gregory Garden with the intention of staying a week and found, four months later, that they had spent the winter there. The house itself was home to Anthony Viegas, his mother, his wife, her sister, four of his brothers and three school-aged daughters. The broad veranda, wood balustraded and hung with coloured lights, served as the restaurant of the hotel. From this veranda you could smell the garden and watch the sea, and be amused by the sight of those who tried to wade across the river at high tide.

Large yuccas grew in the compound and over the years the points of their leaves had been decorated with the whitened shells of hard-boiled eggs. Between these surrealities grew what you'd expect of a garden in that climate: cannas and plumbago and palm trees and a big frangipani. The back of the house was shaded by a mango and a curry tree. Amid the greenery stood four whitewashed buildings which were divided into rooms for the lodgers, each furnished with a bed and a ceiling fan and rented out at sixty rupees a night in the high season. There were more comfortable places to stay, but Nick and Cathy had settled in before they had got their bearings, and the Gregory Garden had come to feel like a second home, a sentiment having more to do with feeling at ease than living in comfort.

By the time they were tackling the veranda steps on that day, Nick had recovered consciousness and regained a little control over himself. Anthony waited at the top, with the knowing grin of someone who has watched his tripping guests return in a similar condition for twenty seasons. He had never been tempted to try a hallucinogen himself.

'Rum pineapple?' he suggested. You never knew whether he was being facetious. 'Chicken garlic sandwich?'

Because those were exactly the things which Nick had been craving, he said, 'Shouldn't we have something else for a change?'

'Don't question a cure that works.' Cathy spoke with the snappishness of an addict whose fix is under threat.

There was a ritual for those detox mornings. They ordered breakfast and bought fresh cigarettes and cold Bisleri water from Anthony, and then retired to their rooms to shower and change and skin up while the food was being assembled.

Once they had absorbed it, the combination of rough alcohol and fresh fruit juice and about a head and a half of raw garlic in each of the sandwiches made the rest of the day seem more like a possibility. Afterwards they went to the hammocks at the back of the house and smoked away the hottest hours. At about four they stirred themselves from a gossiping drowse and checked the tide to see if the river was crossable. Nick would have been happy to stay where he was, but Cathy had made her mind up that they were going, so he traipsed down to the beach after her, hoping that his walk of the living dead might be taken for elegant insouciance.

Once they were there he was glad that she'd forced him to make the effort. They waited for the sunset, waving away the hordes of fruit ladies and lungi merchants, daring each other to swim among the jellyfish, and suffering bouts of inexplicable mirth from behind their sunglasses. When the sun had eased itself behind the sea it was time to schlepp up the sand to Vincent's bar and rejoin society.

Halfway there, just beyond the straggling black line of fishing boats, on an obscenely white towel, wearing sunglasses on the top of his head and a pair of shorts around his middle, sat Aaron Gunn. He had a better body than Nick had expected for one so lanky. Nick thought how unfair it was that some people could look good without having to go to the gym, and decided simultaneously that he was going to do what he could to get this man into bed.

Nick was ready with his most lascivious grin, but then Aaron looked at him, and he was held in that look: more embraced than trapped, made uncomfortable but electrified at the same time. He felt his scrotum contract as though someone were licking at it with a tongue as rough as a cat's. Remembering the condition he had been in at their last meeting, he covered his shame by giving as genteel a sign of greeting as he could muster, and nudged Cathy to make her aware of Aaron's presence.

Cathy said hello to the man as if the word were a fishbone in her throat.

Aaron made the minimum response warranted by civility.

Nick thought he was going to be sick. There was something about the man which was creating a knot in his stomach. There were still a fair number of chemicals loose in his bloodstream and his mind was not clear enough to decide whether this knot was a symptom of fear or of love. He was not someone, in any case, who could have a concept of love which did not involve fear.

When they were out of earshot Nick asked Cathy if she could remember the man's name.

'No,' she said. 'I never asked him.'

'What do you think he does? For a living?'

'Retired prostitute and blackmailer.'

'You don't like him?'

'He has a mouth like an arsehole and he talks shite.'

'He doesn't seem so bad to me.' Nick spoke lamely, to avoid the risk of sounding defensive.

'So I've noticed.' Cathy's tone was the one with which she generally managed to finish a conversation.

They paused in the deep sand at the entrance to Vincent's to check who was there of the people they knew, whether the comfortable chairs had already been taken and whether there was tolerable music in the system. Sensing that Cathy's hand was close by, Nick rubbed his thumb in her palm. She accepted small signs of affection, so long as they were discreetly done.

'I could sleep now,' he said, feeling the length of the trip behind him.

'No you couldn't. I know you. You could close your eyes, but you have another four hours of babbling left in you yet.'

She let him sag against her for a second, then pointed towards Fergus and Andrew, who were sitting on their own with empty chairs alongside them. 'Come on,' she said. 'Deep breaths. The fun doesn't stop for a while yet. You're supposed to be on holiday.'

She kissed Fergus and slapped Andrew on the back as though she were hoping that he had sunburn.

'Well boys,' she said, 'when's the decree nisi?'

Andrew, unable to choose between looking hurt, taking offence or being as amused as everyone else, managed no more than his normal expression of open-mouthed confusion.

'Glad to see you're still taking the Prozac,' Fergus said, as he handed her the joint in his left hand and drew on the one in his right. He was the only person she knew who got away with standing up to her. Cathy smirked as though she had been paid a compliment, while Andrew beamed as if his honour had been defended.

Fergus was the lynchpin of the holiday. He was little and hard and mouthwatering in that sideburns-and-trainers sort of way. The kind of person who was always sorted for gear and made you feel that wherever he was was the place to be. He'd been coming to Goa for years, and it was he who had persuaded Cathy and Nick to come out that winter. Cathy said it was because he couldn't stand the thought of being alone with Andrew. Since the pair had met, about eighteen months beforehand, Fergus and Andrew had been seeing out an entanglement which was patently hopeless to any observer, but which still had a course to run before either of them could quit it with any degree of resolve. Cathy's theory was that Fergus was going to die of boredom before he had a chance to find someone better. If she was unkind to Andrew it might have had something to do with having been guilty of introducing them to each other in the first place. She was frustrated by Fergus' obstinacy in remaining in an unhappy attachment. Andrew, being harmless in himself and more dependent on his physical attractions than his mental resources, was an easy target for her bile. The only real offence he had committed was to fall in love with someone who would, inevitably, tire of him. His big mistake was that the object of this misguided affection was a friend of Cathy's.

As the beach cooled the bar filled. Aaron appeared briefly, wearing a shirt but wet from the waist down, as though he had just been swimming. Nick's eyes locked on to the outline of his dick as he stood, sideways on, at the bar. At first, Nick thought such a public display of near-nakedness was shocking, then he realised that no one else was taking any notice but himself and that it was, in those circumstances, a comparatively modest way to dress, since others were wandering around only in tangas. Aware that people might realise he was staring, he tried to disguise his fixation, but only succeeded in looking shifty, so he put his sunglasses on. Just as he did so, Aaron glanced in his direction. He grinned involuntarily and Aaron creased his eyes in acknowledgement.

'Got a problem?' Cathy asked, tapping on Nick's sunglasses.

Deciding that he wasn't very good at these games of seduction, Aaron drank his beer standing by the bar and left. He couldn't face an evening of sitting on his own and feigning an interest in the mid-distance, waiting for a chance to enter the conversation while pretending that he was indifferent to company. The prospect made him weary, and he thought of having an early night and catching up on sleep from the night before.

Normally, Nick and Cathy would also have had an early night following a party, but Cathy and Fergus were on particularly good form that day, competing to make the bitchiest remarks about anyone who came into view, and then they all somehow found themselves in a taxi going down to Tito's. They were off their trollies by that time, past several thresholds of tiredness, with eyes like muppets and the movements of automatons. They sat in the thickest part of the crowd, at the top of the steps between the bar and the garden. Though Nick's perception was blurred to a vague impression of lights and noises and faces that floated past, disconnected and at random, he did manage to register the fact that Aaron was there.

Cathy confirmed it. 'The sex pest is following you.'

'Who?'

'The lanky one. I hope you're wearing clean knickers in case there's a medical examination after the rape.'

In his hotel room Aaron had been so bludgeoned by loneliness that he couldn't sleep. Such a feeling was rare for him. He was so used to self-sufficiency that he had planned an entire year in his own company without once imagining that such company might be irksome. After two hours of prowling his room and picking at his fingernails he had set out for a walk down the beach in the moonlight. He scanned the people in Vincent's as he passed, and then felt ashamed of himself for being so pathetic. It was as though he had lost control, and over someone he had not yet spoken to. He decided that he needed to set limits on his stay in this limbo. He would book himself out on the next available sleeper. That would probably entail a wait of two or three days, in which time he would have either spoken to the man or come to his senses. Alongside the need he felt to establish some kind of contact with the smiling man called Lovely, he needed to repossess the calmness of mind he had known less than twenty-four hours earlier. 'Cure or kill,' he said to himself, and walked, miserable, towards the lights and music of Tito's, and found himself in a crowd with a beer in his hand.

One minute Nick was dancing and the next he and Aaron were looking at one another, and it occurred to Nick that this was too public a place for something so private as the content of that exchange of looks. He touched Aaron on the elbow and then they were walking through all the people, past his watchdog Cathy who was slumped unconscious on her forearm on the table, down the steps and the slope of plastic chairs full of sunburnt drinkers, through the dunes and out onto the beach, where the moon was in its first night of waning.

Ridiculously, Nick felt that if something didn't happen soon he might cry, and so he stopped walking and inclined his head a little, up towards Aaron's.

It might have been the drugs, and almost certainly the drugs had something to do with it, but though he had been kissed while in a similar condition before, he could not remember anything to compare with this. There was nothing to decide and nothing to control, no awareness of teeth or tongues as physical entities, as though all the parts had already been choreographed and programmed and all that was left for him to do was register the sensations.

They stopped, after a long time, when they heard voices further along the beach, and Nick said, 'What do we do now?'

Aaron said, 'Come around the world with me.'

'I think,' Nick answered, 'we should have a fuck first and see how that works out.'

L ovely was not his real name but something which had stuck from his time as a Blitz Kid. In the days when you could rise to fame by wearing a lot of make-up and talking your way into the right nightclubs, Nick became part of a band called Prêt À Baiser, along with his friends Martin Gale and Prince Albert. They almost got a recording contract, a complete lack of musical ability being no impediment in that era, and might have gone on to stardom, were it not for the unhappy accident that one of the record company employees actually spoke French and pointed out that the band's title did not mean 'Ready To Kiss' as everyone, including the person who had coined it, had previously believed. They offered to change their name, but it was too late: credibility had been lost and there were a thousand other talentless young people who were prepared to wear lip gloss and drop the word *outré* into every sentence, ready to take their place on the New Romantic production line. Martin Gale went on to have his fifteen minutes, miming keyboards for Manual Correction (Deborah Harry was rumoured to have been seen at one of their gigs and, though there was a certain amount of disagreement as to which of their three gigs it was, that earned them a small photograph in the *NME*), but all Nick got out of it was a soubriquet which he found preferable to the name he had been born with, and the useful anecdotal preamble 'When I was with the band, we used to . . .'

These facts, or a version of them which was slightly more favourable to Nick's dignity, were related to Aaron during the first bout of pillow talk which followed their return to the room at the Gregory Garden. They had failed, despite persistent and subtle methods, to persuade Nick's penis to assume any size and shape other than that of a shelled walnut, which was the form it had taken as a result of the extraordinary amount of drugs he had ingested, and so were forced to resort to conversation. Nick asked Aaron what he did, and Aaron said that he wrote, and Nick said that he had often thought of being a writer and that he was sure his life would make a bestseller, and then asked Aaron what he wrote about. When Aaron said, 'Food, mostly,' Nick said 'That rings a bell,' and looked at him closely (the light was on) and asked him what his surname was. Once told, Nick immediately said, 'I know you. You're a panellist on *Cook The Books.*'

'Sometimes,' Aaron said. 'I do other stuff as well.'

'I'm in showbusiness too.'

Aaron thought of saying that he was hardly in showbusiness, but realising that might sound snobbish asked instead, 'Really? What as?'

'Nightclub promotion. That sort of thing. I used to be in a band.'

If Nick told a fib or two that night he might be forgiven. He was erectionless and in bed with someone who was, in his terms, a celebrity, and rampant to boot. That is not to say that he felt inadequate, but he may have been taking precautions to avoid that possibility. One of the drawbacks of sleeping with people you hardly know is that you are inclined to tell them things which, should a relationship develop, you might regret. Nick kept his end up by putting a high gloss on his days of glory, and by naming all the pop stars he was acquainted with and had slept with (and by dissembling made it amount to the same thing), explaining who they were in cases where Aaron was unfamiliar with the names. For all he knew Aaron was a one-night stand, and it wouldn't have done to leave him with the impression that he had slept with someone who was fazed by contact with the famous.

Aaron, for his part, did his best to explain that he was really no more than a jobbing hack. That he had also written other books, under various pseudonyms, on anything from chess to horsebreeding. He admitted that his greatest moneyspinner had been an encyclopaedia of cats. Though modest in intention, this had the effect of making him seem like a one-man publishing industry, and too clever by half.

'You're a very clever man,' Nick said, letting the sentence trail at the end, as though cleverness was not necessarily something to be proud of.

Eventually, in mid-sentence, Nick fell asleep. Aaron tried to stay awake a while longer, to sort out the confusion in his mind. There was something he felt for this man which, in all the times he had thought himself to be in love, he hadn't known before. It was a feeling of calmness, more than anything, which disturbed him. He had the sensation that, in lying beside Nick, he was where he belonged; that the hard part of life was over and he was home. His intelligence told him that nothing could be that simple, but he was too tired to think it through. He fell asleep also, denying his intelligence its last chance to assert itself.

They spent their first days in that room. Nick would emerge, now and again, crossing the garden in a lungi and banyan, to stand on the veranda, with his back to the sea, waiting for Anthony to appear. Sometimes it was for cigarettes or Bisleri, sometimes for food; always for drink. There was whisky in the morning coffee and rum in the evening chocolate and Kingfisher beer at all times in between. They were celebrating having found each other.

It began on the first morning while they were still half asleep. Nick said, 'There's something going on here, isn't there?'

Aaron locked him in his arms and said, 'I think so.'

'Oh good,' Nick said. 'I thought I might be the only one. I thought I was imagining it.' His voice was different, more profound.

'You're not imagining it. There's definitely something going on here.' Aaron was aware that he was exposing himself by admitting it, but he couldn't pretend that he wasn't feeling something, even out of caution. If this was the man he'd been looking for he wanted to start with unequivocal truth.

'We're falling in love, aren't we?'

Aaron wanted to say that he thought so and then, deliberately, chose the word, 'Yes.'

Those were the days when everything had come out right. They knew, for certain, that every action and incident and disaster of their existences had led to this point. Meaning colonised the universe. Concepts like death and infinity, which used to have them shaking in their separate beds if they considered them, no longer had the power of overwhelming. They knew what absolute love was, infinity was within their control, and death was no more than an incident in a progression of events which was fated to have the best of all possible resolutions. They had reached the point where they thought they had earned the right to live happily ever after.

Aaron said, 'If you are the man I think you are, then I have been waiting for you all my life.'

Nick said, 'You are mine now. I can make this last forever.'

One of them must have known that there is nothing more flattering than reciprocated love.

Sometimes Nick would imagine that he was being swallowed by the love, and he would think of a reason to leave the room, but once he was on the veranda he barely spoke, and in the few minutes he would have to wait for whatever Anthony was bringing him, his head would be constantly turning in the direction from which he had come.

On one of these excursions, on the evening of the second day, he found Cathy at a table, eating a thali with a fork. 'Well,' she said, 'how's the shagathon going?'

'It's not like that.'

'Sorry,' she said, without making any effort to sound as though she meant it.

'Don't. Don't be like that. There's something going on here.'

'I should say.'

'You don't have to play the cynical old bitch with this one. I'm a grown man, not a giddy teenager. I know what I'm doing. We both do. I'm practically middle-aged, for Christ's sake. It's about time I got it right.'

'You are thirty-four.' She spoke with a firmness of tone which would not normally be used with anyone over fourteen.

'Old enough to be sick of sleeping with strangers. I know that this is the big one.'

'And what does he have to say?'

Something in the sharpness of her voice penetrated the glaze between them. Nick said, 'You really hate him, don't you?'

'I don't know him. Neither do you, for that matter.'

'I feel as though I do. I feel as though I always knew him. When I saw him at the party it was like recognising someone. More finding than discovering.'

She scanned his eyes to see whether he was under the influence. He was using phrases which were not from his own vocabulary, so he must have been under an influence of some kind. She said, 'When you saw him at the party you thought he was a television.'

There was no answer to that. He watched her flick the cardamoms out of her rice for a few seconds, then announced, 'He's famous.'

She snorted. 'He'd have to have something going for him. As what?'

'He's on the telly. All the time.'

'*Fraggle Rock*, I suppose.'

'You aren't taking this seriously.'

She filled her mouth with food, spent a long time dealing with it, and then changed the subject by asking if he wanted to go to Arambol. Fergus was organising a boat to go in the next day or two. She said, 'You could bring along whatever his name is, I suppose.'

'Aaron.'

'Well?'

'I'll see. I'll ask him.' He had heard a lot about Arambol, but it sounded a bit too much like an expedition. He was comfortable where he was and, with a bit of luck, Aaron would feel the same.

'Suit yourself,' she said. She sounded as if she was giving up on him.

'You're supposed to be my best friend, Cathy. I thought when something like this happened you'd be happy for me. You could make a bit more effort.'

It was taking a risk to sound so petulant with her, but that time it paid off. She stabbed at a lump of dahl and said, 'This come-down's been a shithole. We shouldn't have gone to Tito's.' For a moment she almost sounded apologetic. 'And,' she said, 'I've spent half the bloody day drinking that stinking whisky and listening to that suicidal Austrian with the dreads.'

'The one in the leatherette hat?'

'In the end I told him he had a straightforward choice between topping himself and washing himself, and that the shock of soap and water would probably kill him in any case.'

'You never did.'

'I wish people like that would just get on with it. It bores the tits off me when they're all talk and no Gillette.'

'So you don't mind about Aaron really? You'll give him a chance?'

'I think it's happening a bit too quickly. You only met him yesterday and already you're ordering the bridesmaids' frocks. I know what you can be like and I know who has to pick up the pieces.'

'It won't be like that this time. With something this big you know when you've got it right. And we've talked about all that already and how we're going to make it work. We've both been around enough to know what the pitfalls are. It's still sinking in that we've found each other.'

'Soppy cunt,' she said.

Across the compound, a shadow moved between the room and the lavatory. Nick felt his insides tighten and a sneaking sense of unreality. Cathy's face was red and yellow in the coloured lights. For the first time since he had known her she looked as though she might be tactful.

'When you boys are finished with the honeymoon of the century,' she said, 'perhaps we can all be a little more sociable. Do you think you'll make it to Arambol?'

'I'll ask. We'll see.'

Nick was on his feet and restless. Anthony brought the drinks he had come for. He smiled a sort of apology at Cathy and was on his way down the steps, and along the path among the yuccas. The speared eggshells, picked out in the moonlight, appeared to be floating in the thickness of the air.

The room smelled of Odomos and cocoa butter and Bombay black, a combination as rich and pungent as the smell of a Christmas pudding. It was only in Nick's brief absences that Aaron would become aware of his surroundings. There was no window. In the daytime the light seeped between gaps in the rooftiles. At night there was a bare lightbulb of token wattage – sometimes. Often the power failed and a candle was lit. When there was electricity the ceiling fan circled on the slowest and quietest speed, making eddies across the mosquito net. There was always the sound of the sea, drowned in the evening by the purr of insects. The room was small and the bed took up half of it. A weedy-looking chair, half-hidden in mounds of cloth and clothing, was the nearest substitute for a wardrobe. The basin and shower cubicle were concrete, and a concrete surface projected from the wall at table height, painted, like the floor, the colour of dried blood. Everywhere was packed with clutter, with the sort of senseless objects that Aaron had excluded from his own travelling bag. These things – clothes, sunglasses, cigarette lighters, medicines, grooming equipment, bottles of aftershave, shoes and boots, pictures of Krishna bought from street vendors, magazines, personal stereo and cassettes, camera and films, Tibetan bracelets, airline freebies, joss sticks and rolls of lavatory paper – were scrutinised and handled by Aaron as if they contained information about his new lover. He wanted to know, in detail, all there was to know. In the same way as, when Nick was with him, he studied every pore and line and hair of his body, curious and fascinated. Had Aaron been able, in any practical sense, to think of himself for a moment, he would have seen that his whole mind had been taken over but, because the mania was complete, there was no room for any thought which might question his obsession.

There was, on the other hand, half an hour when Nick was left alone while Aaron went back to his hotel to pay something on account, and assure the management that he had not done a bunk. Nick thought that he would take the opportunity to tidy up a little and sort out some laundry, but the novelty of having some time to himself was too much for him, so he thought he'd just roll a little joint first, and enjoy the clear air of solitude.

Nick had a problem being as intense as Aaron was, all the time; with the way Aaron kept uncovering his body and running his hand over it.

'Don't,' Nick would say. 'I'm getting fat.'

'I think you're beautiful.'

'You should have seen me a couple of years ago, when I was going to the gym.'

'I wouldn't have you any different.'

'I'll start working out again, as soon as we get back.'

'You don't need to. Not for me.'

Nick would give Aaron's tit a squeeze and say, 'It wouldn't do you any harm either.'

Aaron would look so worried that it made Nick laugh.

'Do you think I'm too skinny?'

'There's always room for improvement.'

Nick, in fact, thought that Aaron had an almost perfect body, but it amused him to see how frail an ego could be, in intimate circumstances; how you only had to look at someone in a certain way, even someone like Aaron, to see the seeds of self-doubt germinate on their face.

As Nick stubbed the roach out in the ashtray something white and half-concealed caught his eye. It was Aaron's Calvins, which he hadn't bothered to wear as he was going to be away for such a short amount of time. Nick found himself picking them up as though they were something breakable. For a minute he stroked the crotch with his thumbs, and then he pressed them into his face as though the cotton were oxygen and he was in need of it. He became aware that he had an erection, for the first time since before the party. They had done things, all sorts of things, but for him it had been, in effect, thirty-six hours of foreplay with no result. Aaron had been the one who'd supplied all the sperm which had made the small towel as stiff as cardboard. The 'I'm always like this after taking drugs' excuse was beginning to wear a bit thin, even though Aaron was showing no signs of disbelief or resentment. Nick, delighted by this sudden return of potency, put his hand down without having to think once about it and, with a mouth full of slightly soiled gusset, set about making up for lost time.

At the sound of the latch he had only a moment to drop the underpants back onto the floor, roll on his stomach to hide the erection and pretend to be dozing. Although he should have been flattered that Aaron had hurried back so quickly, he couldn't help feeling that his privacy had been invaded and that it was a bit much that he hadn't even been given time for a decent wank. This falling in love business was all very well, but it was obvious that they were going to need a little time to themselves. It wasn't normal to be spending every minute of the day and night together. As far as Nick was concerned, they had done all the bonding and said everything they needed to say to each other for the moment, but Aaron seemed very clingy and it would be hard to think of a way of getting rid of him for a few hours without offending him.

After the sound of the door opening and closing there was silence for a long time, and Nick began to think that Aaron must have gone out again. He opened an eye to check and saw Aaron standing over him, saying nothing, but staring at him in a way which he found slightly creepy.

'What's the matter?'

'You're very beautiful when you're asleep. I didn't want to disturb you.'

'Too late.'

Aaron said that he was sorry. He apologised easily, whether he had been the offender or not.

The erection had not subsided, and Nick thought it was a shame to waste it, so he rolled over. 'Surprise,' he said.

While Aaron got on with the business of familiarising himself with the new state of things, Nick watched the top of his head and thought how much he was looking forward to being at home again; to dating Aaron in the way that a normal couple would, seeing each other three or four times a week and having sex when they were desperate for each other, instead of all this constant feeling and snogging. They had discovered that, by a stroke of luck, they lived in the same area. They even went to the same club occasionally, a place called Priapus. When he found out, Aaron had thought that it was extraordinary they hadn't met before. He had held Nick's face in his hands and said, 'How could I have missed you? You were right under my nose all the time. When I think of all the years I wasted not knowing you.'

Nick had let his mind wander and the long-awaited erection dissolved without a conclusion.

'Sorry,' Aaron said, blaming himself again.

A little later Nick asked, 'Are you bored?'

'No. I've never had such a nice time in my life. Why? Are you?'

'There isn't anything you feel you should be doing.'

'No. I should be getting on a train. I didn't mean to stay here long, but there's nowhere else I have to be. Goa doesn't seem so bad all of a sudden.'

Aaron leaned forward to emphasise the point with a kiss, but Nick ducked him and said, 'Skin up for me, sweetheart. You're so much better at it than I am.'

Watching the concentration on Aaron's face as he rolled the joint, Nick realised how much he was in love, and that everything he had said about that was probably true. He decided that he could spend the rest of his life with Aaron, loving only him. Aaron was the sort of man he needed: good enough to look after him and attractive enough to keep him interested. Nick said, without thinking, 'I don't know what I'll do when you have to leave.'

'Come with me.'

Nick wasn't going to admit that he didn't have the money to go swanning round the world on a whim, unlike some people. 'I can't,' he said. 'I have commitments I can't get out of. There are all sorts of things set up for when I get back. People depending on me.'

'Business?' Aaron asked. He sounded cautious, because any other time he had tried to get Nick to be specific about his job the answer had been, 'Can we not talk about work all the time? I'm supposed to be on holiday. I came here to get away from all that. I really needed this holiday. Don't spoil it for me.'

This time Nick just answered, 'Yes,' briskly, and changed

the subject by asking Aaron if he wanted to go to Arambol the next day.

'How?'

'Fergus is organising a boat. Everyone's going.' Nick realised that this was going to be one of those ideas which sounded better the more he talked about it. 'I should go,' he said. 'I've been neglecting my friends. We should start being sensible. The rest of our lives doesn't have to stop just because we're in love.'

'Fine.'

Nick got a rush of energy at the thought of escaping from the lethargy and claustrophobic love-junketing of the previous few days. He began to tidy the room, waving the joint about and talking at the same time. 'Don't just sit there,' he said. 'Help me with this.'

Aaron looked about him doubtfully. He couldn't see anything that couldn't be done by one person in five minutes flat. A second would only get in the way. He picked a couple of shirts off the floor and stood holding them, unsure where they could be put down again.

'You're hopeless.' Nick took the shirts from him. 'Look, if you want to be useful you could take some stuff to the laundry for me, in Calingute. I'll meet you back at your hotel in an hour or so.'

It did not occur to Aaron that there could be any objection to this suggestion. He went to Calingute, complying with no more reservation than if he had been asked to go up to the veranda. In his experience people would not ask you to do something unless there was a very good reason why they couldn't do it themselves. He was not to know that, in Nick's system of relationships, you only did something yourself if everyone you knew had flatly refused to do it for you. Had Aaron, at that early moment, told Nick to fuck off and carry his own laundry, he would have earned a certain amount of respect. As it was, he only earned himself a wasted journey, since the laundry was closed by the time he got there. He did, however, buy Nick a silver box from the Tibetans instead, in compensation for having failed the task.

Once Aaron was out of the way, Nick showered and changed and went off to find Fergus to book the two of them on the trip. He had so much news to tell everyone that he lost track of the time and it was getting on for eleven when he arrived at the hotel. Aaron behaved as though he'd been gone a month. Seeing him sway a little in the doorway, Aaron rushed forward, asking if he was all right. He helped Nick to the bed and unbuttoned his shirt, and it was not until he smelled the whisky fumes that he registered the cause of Nick's skewed grin.

'Come here,' Nick said, pulling Aaron down on him. 'Do you know how happy I am? How happy you're making me?'

All Aaron could say was, 'Where were you? I couldn't think what had happened to you. I even went back to the Gregory to find out if you were there.'

'The shackles on already, darling?'

'No. I was worried. That's all.'

'Well I'm here now. Aren't you pleased?'

'Yes,' Aaron admitted. 'Relieved. I thought you'd had an accident or something.'

'I was telling everyone about you. How clever and famous you are.'

'I'm not famous.'

'It's nothing to be ashamed of. I'm proud of you.'

'Famous means that you don't have to tell people who you are. Getting your name in the paper from time to time doesn't qualify.'

His quibbling was making Nick feel tired. 'I don't think we should argue about it.' Nick closed his eyes and reached for the cigarettes.

'I don't want you to get the wrong idea about me.'

'That's up to you,' Nick said, archly. 'I can only go by what you tell me. I want to know everything.'

'Like what?'

'We can't have secrets between us.'

'We don't.' Aaron sounded puzzled. 'I don't.'

'If we are going to spend the rest of our lives together there has to be complete honesty. This isn't going to work unless we make it work.'

'I know that,' Aaron said. 'I would have thought that all that was understood.'

'Well it needs to be said. And I mean it. I've been in a lot of relationships that broke up because of lies and secrecy. I don't have the energy to go through all that again. This is my last chance for happiness and I'm not going to let you wreck it.'

Nick seemed to be on the verge of tears and, though Aaron didn't quite see what he was getting at, he could see that the man was in need of comfort. He propped Nick in the crook of his arm and talked to him, stroking his hair as he did so.

Nick wasn't aware of many of the other things that were said that night. He heard Aaron telling him about his background and family and stuff, and life in the Gunn household, but he was drifting in and out of a doze in the way you do when you've had a skinful. Occasionally Aaron would ask him if he were sleeping and he'd deny it. It was nice to hear the sound of Aaron's voice, like being told a bedtime story. There was a lot about growing up in the country and horses and schools and university. Things that meant nothing to Nick but, all the same, he began to feel that if he could become part of Aaron's life he could somehow achieve all that stability by proxy. He lost consciousness completely when Aaron got to the bit about being a thrusting young journalist. Aaron had made his life sound so secure and worthwhile and reasonable that he felt safe with him. Nick was seduced. Until that moment the nearest Nick Lovely had ever got to a feeling of safety was in his frequent bouts of oblivion.

Aaron lay still for a long time, putting up with the cramp in his arm, until he was sure that Nick was sleeping too soundly to be woken by disturbance. There was a lot of thinking to be done. He had understood, from the way Nick had spoken, that the man's experience of life had not been the best. It was hard for him to imagine anyone being vile or abusive to Nick, but he was aware that these things happened. He knew, was absolutely certain, that he loved Nick enough to make up for anything in the past. He got his first inkling that his role in Nick's life might involve more than making a future together. It could be that there were problems to be overcome first. Never having failed before in anything he had set out to do, he believed, without yet knowing what those problems might be, that he was the man to overcome them.

His diary lay on the bedside table. He had not made an entry for three days.

If there was one thing that Nick couldn't stand, it was people who were energetic in the mornings. They had to get up at an unholy hour to catch Fergus' boat and, instead of grumbling and crawling out of bed like a reasonable person, Aaron bounced. He gargled, he sang in the shower, he tried to rouse Nick with his hair dripping and skin scrubbed clean enough to make a man with a hangover sick, when all Nick needed was paracetamol, a Bloody Mary and another four hours' sleep.

'We're going to be late,' he said.

Nick asked to be left alone, told him that they could get a taxi and catch up with everyone at Arambol, but Aaron wasn't having it. Because Nick was too hungover to argue they made it to the beach on time, Nick groaning and Aaron laughing at him, skipping around like Shirley Temple on orange squash.

The boat terrified Nick. It was a sort of hollow log with bits sticking out of one side, and he crouched in the middle beside Cathy, who was a mine of stories about the number of Goan fishermen who lost their lives at sea. Aaron sat up on the prow with his legs dangling over the edge, chattering with Fergus and pointing out dolphins. Nick wasn't in the mood for dolphins at first, but there were some skilled workers aboard who could roll a spliff in any conditions, and he was soon calm enough to be taking photographs of distant triangles of grey fin, and telling everyone how enamoured he was of nature and how watching Flipper used to make him cry when he was little.

Being cut off, Arambol was free of hawkers and package tourists and you could do, more or less, what you liked. Germans, the shape and colour of strips of biltong, sat naked on the beach, and there was a sort of lake just behind, where people coated themselves in mud and baked in the sun. Fergus ignored all of that, and led his party beyond, down a track that wound into the jungle. He said that they were going to the tree, but when Nick asked what the tree was, he just said that it was 'The Tree', and that they'd see when they got there. Nick, stumbling along the rough path, kept threatening to go back on his own to the bar he'd spotted, clinging to the cliffside. He was, in fact, too frightened of walking through the jungle on his own to do so. Aaron was treating his complaints as a sort of running joke, there being little to complain of, and Nick felt that there was nothing he could do but go on, without looking silly. It seemed that everyone was enjoying themselves except him.

The tree, it transpired, was not so much a tree as the mausoleum of a tree long dead. Once, there must have been a dendrological thing, growing from the rock with a thick, straight bole, rooted in stone and reaching above the canopy of the jungle, a beacon of invincibility in an environment where all other living things struggled for survival. Somehow, a creeper had wound itself around this tree and, for a time, they must have grown together, entwined like lovers, the stronger lifting the other into the light, legs enmeshed and arms spreading over the rival vegetation. When the point of equality was past, the creeper may have acted like a buttress, shoring up the host which it was slowly killing. By the time the tree was dead and rotted away, the creeper had become a mould, an enormous, hollow lattice, hardened into a tube, on immense, erupting roots which broke the very stone they grew from.

There was a flat space, about nine feet in diameter, among these sepulchral roots. Mats had been laid on the stone, and incense burned as in a temple, the victorious parasite soaring above like a goparum, its knees and crevices made into shrines where chillums had been placed by devotees for the use of pilgrims. There was a quiet about the place, more like the stillness found in churches than the hustle of an Indian temple. The ruling deity was marijuana.

Shoes were removed, and new arrivals sat among the small congregation and joined in the rhythmic, wordless lighting and passing of chillums. Anyone who found their hands free for a moment would roll a joint. One or two, who were tripping, stood at the periphery, staring out into the jungle and up at the sky with unaccountable smiles across their faces. Occasionally someone would climb through the hollow centre of the trunk, to emerge and sit in the sunshine, forty feet above the heads of the others.

After a while, when a plateau of anaesthesia had been reached, and the novelty of it wore off, someone produced a bucket of water and a Bisleri bottle. The bottom was cut from the plastic bottle and it was sunk, upright, in the water. A chillum was fitted into the neck and the bottle drawn up, filling with thick white smoke as it rose. The idea was that you whipped the chillum away and put your mouth to the neck and pushed the bottle to the bottom of the bucket with one movement, forcing a litre of smoke into your lungs. Nick thought it was fantastic; even better than a bhang lassi. Aaron refused when his turn came, saying that he smoked to relax, not to become semi-conscious. Nick, though halfway to a coma himself, thought that this sounded a little prissy, and would have been embarrassed by his lover's attitude had he been capable of any sensibility at all.

For a while he was so out of it that he couldn't make out

what anyone was saying, then he became aware that Aaron was talking to Andrew about climbing through the trunk.

'Don't,' Nick said.

'Why?'

'I've got a bad head for heights. I won't be able to stomach it.'

'You don't have to come,' Aaron said.

Nick said that he had no intention of coming; that he had meant he wouldn't be able to watch. Aaron looked at him as though he had said something ridiculous, and Nick was stoned enough to think that he probably had. The next thing he was conscious of was Aaron and Andrew squeezing themselves through the hollow. They were lost from sight for a while and then appeared at the top, calling down through the leaves that the view was incredible and the others didn't know what they were missing.

Sickened and dizzied, as he had predicted, Nick had to stop watching. He held on to Cathy's arm as though he were the one in danger. 'They're going to fall off and die,' he said. Cathy laughed. She could think of no better solution to the fixes her friends had got themselves into. She embarked on a little fantasy about seeing Nick and Fergus through their grief until they all became the happy triumvirate they had once been.

'Just my luck,' Nick said, 'to fall in love and become a widower all in the same week.' He was trying to make a joint, but his hands were shaking so badly that the papers wouldn't stick.

'D'ya love him then?' Cathy asked.

Nick thought that he was being addressed, and was about to answer when he heard Fergus say, 'Why?' and realised that the question had not been directed his way. Cathy and Fergus were both staring up at the branches, where Aaron and Andrew appeared to be in conversation.

'Because,' she said, as though she were explaining

something tiresomely obvious, 'there couldn't be any other reason for putting up with him.'

'He's got a nice dick.'

'The dick hasn't been built that could make up for a personality like that.'

'He means well.'

'You haven't answered.'

'I do,' Fergus said. 'I love him.' He made the words themselves sound like burdens.

'So, when are you going to dump him?'

Fergus didn't answer. The problem he was having with Andrew was a fairly straightforward one, which was all the more reason for not subjecting it to Cathy's prejudiced scrutiny. Fergus wanted to open up their relationship, while Andrew was committed to the practice of monogamy. Any other differences between them had arisen out of this, fundamental, conflict. Cathy, with her irrational dislike of Andrew, was not an ideal arbiter.

She said, 'You want to get out of it? Right?'

'Does that seem obvious?'

She clucked irritably. 'Don't annoy me with stupid questions. I sometimes think men were designed to make the rest of us look clever. You want out and you still love him, so you're probably still shagging each other senseless, which is the only thing that's holding you together, apart from the fact that you're being too nice and you don't want to hurt him.'

'Fine,' he said, in token capitulation rather than agreement.

'Well then?'

'Well what?'

'You have a straightforward choice. You can be miserable for the rest of your life because you don't have the guts to get rid of him, or you can dump him and make him miserable for the short amount of time it'll take him to get over you.'

'Short amount of time?' There was a note of self-mockery in Fergus' affronted tone.

'He may have told you that he can't live without you, but we've all said that and believed it at the time. You may like the idea of being indispensible, but he'll soon sort himself out. There's not much room for a long memory in that little head.'

'It's not as simple as that.'

'The longer you hang around him,' she said, 'the more likely he is to think that he's got you for life.'

'Well maybe he has.'

Though they were speaking in a low tone, they were talking freely, as though no one else was in hearing range. Indeed, all the others were so stoned that they each seemed in a world of their own, outwardly oblivious to anything but the next chillum or joint put into their hands. Nick, however, found himself listening carefully. He wanted to say something but he was so out of his box that he couldn't make his mouth work.

At first, he thought he was experiencing *déjà vu*, but then he realised that the feeling of familiarity came from the fact that he had been subjected to this selfsame lecture from Cathy, more than once. These were her standard lines, her guaranteed reaction to every relationship he had ever had. Cathy did not believe in love. She was never going to accept that it was worth sorting out a few problems for the sake of long-term happiness. Nick found himself wanting to shout her down; to tell Fergus to stick with it, that whatever was going on between him and Andrew was no one's business but their own. He knew that if he and Aaron were to stay together he would face this same diatribe from Cathy.

Fergus, turned hypothetical by the force of Cathy's arguments, was saying, 'How do you suggest I do it, then?'

'Please. You're a grown boy. You shouldn't need to be told how to do these things. Just tell him. Or let him see you with your gob around someone else's knob. Or pack your bags and leave a cruel little note pinned to the valance. Don't pretend that you haven't spent half your waking hours working out the best way to drop the little pet.'

'You're a tactless woman.'

'But I'm right. Aren't I?'

Fergus said nothing. For a long time he stayed in the same squatting position, his feet flat on the ground and his knees tucked into his armpits, looking up towards where Andrew was sitting in the foliage. He took a pull on a chillum which had just been handed to him, but it must have gone down the wrong way and he began to cough his guts up.

Nick found his voice and said, 'That isn't fair,' but, as no one was inclined to think that the remark could be addressed to themself, he was ignored. The things which Cathy had been saying to Fergus had left Nick with a vision of Aaron in the arms of another man. It was making him sick and angry with jealousy. He did not know how to express this; how to tell Cathy that he had every intention of staying with Aaron and that she had better keep her nose out of the relationship. The words which formed themselves out of his frustration and were said aloud were, 'I'd kill him. I'd kill him before I'd let him go with someone else.'

There seemed to be nothing anyone could add to that.

High in the canopy, Andrew and Aaron were having a far pleasanter time. They had begun with a long and passionate discussion about cats, disagreeing only because Andrew was inclined towards the oriental varieties, while Aaron had a penchant for the long-haired. They finally settled on the Birman as an ideal compromise and only then did they move on to the subject of love. Andrew said that he and Fergus were more in love now than they were in the beginning, and that things got better all the time. He admitted that they'd had their ups and downs, but said that every up was higher than the one which went before, and every down of less significance. Aaron felt very naive, at first, to be getting what amounted to advice from someone who was almost ten years his junior, but Andrew seemed like an expert on the subject of making relationships last. Andrew declared that trust was the main thing: you had to take responsibility for your love by trusting your lover absolutely and without question. If you were with someone you couldn't trust then you were with the wrong man.

'Am I?' Aaron asked.

'Are you what?'

'Am I with someone I can trust? You've known him for a while.'

Andrew considered before answering, then said, 'I think so. I don't know him that well. He's Fergus' friend really. But I like him. I think he's in love with you. I know it hasn't been long, but I've never seen him like this before. He's obviously crazy about you. He needed someone like you. Normally he goes for complete bastards. It's time he had someone nice. You'll bring the best out in him.'

Aaron's face turned red at the compliment, then he said, 'Fuck it. I've torn my shirt.' He had noticed the rip a while before, but now seemed an appropriate time to mention it, rather than have to think of a response to Andrew's agony-uncling. 'It must have happened coming up through the tree.' He decided to throw the shirt down to Nick rather than worsen the rip on the way back.

When Nick heard his name called he looked up to see Aaron moving slowly, like a chameleon on a branch, until he was standing upright on the bough. Nick screwed his eyes closed, terrified that Aaron might fall, and so didn't see him take his shirt off. Aaron called again and the next thing that Nick saw was the deep, irridescent blue of the shirt tumbling through the air. Mistaking one of Aaron's shirts for something else for the second time, Nick thought it was the man himself, and that Aaron had fallen out of the tree and was about to land on his face. Nick screamed, and went on screaming for a long time after the cloth draped itself over his head. Naturally, everyone else thought it was hysterically amusing.

For the rest of that day, every so often, Cathy, with a completely straight face, would call out Nick's name. When he'd turn around, she'd yell, 'EEK!' and the others would laugh like drains. It was the funniest thing since magic mushrooms.

Aaron never laughed. He could see how upset Nick was. It was hard for Nick to remain angry with the only person who was prepared to take him seriously and be sympathetic, so he began to forgive Aaron for the incident, though he thought it best not to let his indulgence show.

If Fergus was quiet for the remainder of the day, it wasn't remarked on or interpreted as sullenness. Arambol wasn't a place where a long bout of taciturnity seemed unnatural. Andrew, on the other hand, became quite chatty. His conversation with Aaron in the treetops had made him feel as though he had an ally in the group, and gave him the sort of confidence which Cathy would normally have been able to quash. Then Fergus said that he was going for a walk, adding the word, 'Alone', as Andrew began to scramble to his feet. Andrew's face, as the slapping noise of Fergus' chappels receded along the jungle path, bore an expression more often found on yellow labradors, torn between obedience and desire.

They rode back to Baga on a high sea. Storm clouds obscured the setting sun and the breakers were rolling too hard and fast for the laden boat to land on the beach. There was a sea-sickened silence among the passengers as the nose of the craft was pointed up the river and, by deftness and luck, brought between the pointed rocks which they glimpsed momentarily in the hollow of water which preceded each rearing wave. Some, watching the nearness of the shoreline, computed their chances of swimming through the rough water should the worst happen. Others, chief among them Nick, were convinced that death was imminent, and would not have been ashamed to say so if fear and nausea had not deprived them of the power of speech.

It was only after they were safely on the riverbank that he found his voice. One by one, they had had to leap from the instability of the gunwale, across two or three feet of seething water. Nick was the last to jump, nearly missing his footing through nervousness, but caught, one arm apiece, by Aaron and Fergus. His face was a pale green colour and his hands were shaking. 'I need a drink.'

They were all cold and some were wet and the roughness of the boat ride had somehow knocked the sociability out of them, and the party broke up. When the Gregory was reached, Nick made straight for his room, despatching Aaron to the veranda to get him a triple rum and Coke. He said the word triple several times, in case Aaron might think he was exaggerating his need.

When Aaron brought the drink to the room he found Nick lying face-down on the bed. When the glass was put in his hand he raised himself on his elbows and swallowed half of it without grimacing, before adding Coke to the remainder.

'At least they know what a decent measure is in this country,' he said. A triple rum, when poured by Anthony, amounted to about a third of a pint.

'Better now?' Aaron asked.

The words and the rum together broke whatever dam was holding back the tide of Nick's emotions. Throwing himself on Aaron, he wept torrents. He said he had never been so afraid in his life. At first Aaron thought he was talking about their dodgy landing, until Nick howled, 'Promise, promise, promise me you'll never climb a tree again.'

Since there was no place for reason in the discussion, Aaron had to make the promise. He had never before been the object of such concern, and he had no idea how to deal with it. He dredged his brain for words of reassurance and managed to slot those he found into the occasional few seconds when Nick was pulling on the rum and Coke.

'Come on,' Aaron said. 'Nothing's as bad as all that.'

'You don't know. You've no idea. It's all right for you: you're not afraid of anything. You've no idea what it's like to be me. You just go charging up trees and if you fall out and break your neck your worries are over. I'm the one who's left behind, on my own. I want to spend the rest of my life with you. It's not fair. You're not to die. You're not to.' What had begun as an admission of vulnerability was sounding more like a temper tantrum. Nick's face had the look of a spoilt child.

'What can I do?' Aaron asked, helplessly.

'You can get me another drink for a start.' Nick held his empty glass out. 'A triple. Don't forget,' he added, when Aaron was halfway out of the door.

The thoughts which entered Aaron's head, as he made his way to the veranda, were not welcome. There was something which he found ugly in Nick's high emotion. He told himself that he was imagining it, that they were both tired after the long day, that Nick had had too much to smoke and a couple of bad frights, and the best thing to do would be to get to sleep as quickly as possible. Things would be back to normal in the morning. By this reasoning he decided that Nick had been absolutely right in demanding a stiff drink, and that he should have one himself. By the time he was returning with both his hands full he had made sense of the whole thing. The height of Nick's emotion was in direct proportion to the depth of his love. Aaron turned sentences over in his mind, trying to find one which would let Nick know that his feelings were just as extreme, despite the calmness with which he found himself expressing them.

Nick became quieter with the second drink and was virtually reasonable by the time he had finished off Aaron's glass. He said that he was sorry and that he wasn't proud of himself and that he just needed to be loved, and would Aaron just hold him so that he could feel safe? He was shaking when he asked that, so Aaron held him and told him that there was nothing to be afraid of, and that way they both fell asleep.

There was a clean smell in the air on the morning after the squall. Nick seemed so full of energy and goodwill that, were it not for the glasses and cola bottles by the side of the bed, Aaron might have doubted his memory of the previous night. They even had sex without brushing their teeth, which was not something that bothered Aaron, but Nick had, several times, declared his disgust for early morning snogging. When they were wiping the spunk out of their chest hair, Aaron said, 'About last night.'

'I need a piss,' Nick said. 'Badly. Do you think there's anyone in the loo?' Without waiting for an answer, he said, 'Oh fuck it,' and began to piss in the sink.

'You were pretty upset,' Aaron said.

'Was I?'

'Do you want to talk about it?'

Nick let out a big sigh as the pressure eased on his bladder. Then he said, 'You don't have to make such a drama about it. People get upset from time to time. We can't all be perfect like you.'

'I love you,' Aaron said.

'I know. You don't have to tell me every five minutes. We can love each other without being neurotic about it.'

Aaron said he was sorry.

'Well,' Nick said, 'just try not to overreact in future.'

He was talking so flippantly that he might have been making a joke of his own hysteria, as a cover for any embarrassment he might have felt. Aaron didn't think that he could pursue the matter without seeming petulant. At the same time he had a nagging feeling that he had done something wrong; that Nick's outburst the night before had been his fault, and that Nick was being magnanimous in refusing to discuss it.

'Come on,' Nick said. 'Get dressed. Honeymoon's over. Time we got out and about.'

In fact, they didn't get much further than the veranda that day. Breakfast somehow ran into lunch, and then Nick said that it was too hot to go to the beach. There was a constant dropping-by of people he knew, and he talked the morning away, turning his Arambol experiences to good account. Even the incident of the shirt falling from the tree was honed into a funny story, told at his own expense, always including the line, 'I was scared shitless. I'm not proud of it, but I don't mind telling you. That's just the way I am.'

By the end of the morning Aaron began to see why Nick had so many friends. He talked to anyone who was within reach of his voice. He didn't wait for an opportune moment, the way most people would, he just included strangers in the conversation as though they were old acquaintances who happened to be sitting at a nearby table. Almost everyone responded well to this open-handed treatment. The few who showed reserve were dismissed, after their departure, as 'Stuck-up bastards. Some people just don't know how to be friendly.'

Aaron, who couldn't see how anyone could fail to be charmed by Nick, was inclined to agree.

They were pleasantly drunk and in high spirits when they went out that evening. First they showered and shaved and dressed, grooming each other like cats from the same litter, dealing with the hair in each other's ears and rubbing in

Odomos, and pausing frequently for small caresses. They went through Nick's pile of clothing and found enough white stuff for them both to dress in it from head to toe (although Aaron had to wear a white lungi because all Nick's trousers were too short for him). It looked, when they had finished, as though they had disguised themselves as angels, and they shimmered through the blackness of Baga Bridge and the maze of cafes and Kashmiri souvenir shops. Their progress was slowed by the number of puppies they encountered, every one of which had to be picked up and petted by Nick. Aaron kept thinking that he was going out with the best-natured man he had ever met. The night before was long forgotten.

Eventually they came to their destination, where they found Cathy presiding, at her usual table, over a small but loyal troop. They sat in the two remaining spaces at the end. Cathy smiled at them, and winked at Nick. He could see what she was thinking: if they were coming out of their lair two days in a row, then the peak of the holiday romance might be past and the end of the entanglement in sight. Every time Nick had found someone and introduced him to Cathy her reaction had been the same: she would throw her eyes heavenward and say, 'Not again.' Every time things had gone wrong, her first words of comfort had been, 'It was never going to work. I tried to tell you that from the start.'

Though he had to admit that she had been right in all the other cases, Nick decided that the time had come to prove Cathy wrong. He asked Tina, the Danish girl who was sitting beside her, if she would mind swapping places for a bit.

Aaron looked at Nick as if he had just announced that he was going into a monastery and not to the other end of the table.

'We're not joined at the hip,' Nick said. 'I have to be allowed to see my friends.'

Aaron's mouth broke into a quick, shamefaced smile. 'Sorry,' he said. 'Don't be long.'

Nick was aware that Aaron was watching him as he made his way around the table to sit between Cathy and Fergus. Although Aaron had begun talking to Andrew he was all the while glancing and smiling in Nick's direction, without interrupting the flow of his conversation. Nick couldn't help thinking how much he enjoyed being loved, and of the confidence it gave him to have a man like that at his back, someone handsome and clever and worth being seen with in public.

Fergus clinched it by asking Nick if he and Aaron were in love.

Nick nodded, and said, 'It's looking good.'

Cathy was unable to repress a snort. 'Some people never learn,' she said.

'Don't,' Fergus said.

'Don't what?' She assumed an expression of mock innocence.

'If you're always that cynical about everyone it makes it hard to take you seriously.'

'Don't say you've been taking me seriously.'

Fergus' face was set like granite. He and Andrew had been fighting the night before and he had found himself, in the heat of the moment, quoting some of Cathy's blunter opinions on the subject of love in general and Andrew's delusions of it in particular. Now he spoke to Cathy in an angry, low voice, and with the desperation of someone who realises that he may have made a mistake.

'Haven't you ever been in love?' he asked her. 'Haven't you ever wanted that? Haven't you ever looked at someone and seen what he has inside him and loved him for it, and haven't you thought about not being alone and having someone you can trust as much as you trust yourself? Is that why you can't give anyone else a chance?'

Cathy's facial muscles were not used to astonishment, and so the transformation they underwent might have been interpreted as a symptom of anything from toothache to sudden idiocy. She looked as though she was being buggered with an ice lolly.

Nick tried to lighten things up by saying that Cathy had had a relationship once but had to give it up because the RSPCA were threatening to prosecute, but his joke fell flat and had the two of them glaring at him. He was saved by the waiter, who came for his order.

Because they had arrived late, and everyone else had been halfway through their meal and the restaurant was running low on food, Nick had to settle for a calamari stir-fry. Aaron said that he wasn't very hungry and would just have pudding with everyone else. Negotiating his order took Nick so long that Cathy and Fergus had cooled off and were behaving themselves again by the time he had finished.

By way of apology, Cathy said to Fergus, 'You should know me by now.'

'I suppose,' he said.

'I meant what I said in Arambol. If you've done something about it, it's for the best in the long run. I wouldn't worry.'

'I suppose,' he said.

'He doesn't seem too put out by it, in any case.' She indicated Andrew with a movement of her head. He was deep in conversation with Aaron.

'Just leave it,' Fergus said.

Nick, tired of being talked across, interrupted again, this time pitching his contribution so that it was more in keeping with the general tone. 'Nobody's asking me what I think,' he said sulkily.

They both looked at him as though he had dribble on his chin. He was left wondering why, if the subject was none of his business, they were discussing it so freely under his nose.

The arrival of his food gave him something else to consider. He poked at the warm, greasy pile with his fork for a few seconds, before deciding that he was too hungry for gastronomical quibbling. Although it tasted a bit odd, he put that down to the awkward atmosphere at his end of the table, and so carried on munching his way through the rice and twice-cooked fish and teeming bacilli. At one point he called out to Aaron to ask if he wanted some, but Aaron only shook his head and gave Nick one of those looks that turned his spine liquid and made the back of his skull prickle. Nick munched on, full of love. 'It's your own funeral if you starve,' he said, secretly relieved that Aaron had refused because he disliked anyone else eating from his plate, no matter how much he liked to think he was in love.

'The funeral might be yours,' Cathy muttered, looking disdainfully at what remained on his plate.

He polished it off with defiance. It was only then that he remembered why he had come to this end of the table in the first place. He had a little campaign to wage on his lover's behalf.

'So,' he said. 'What do you think of Aaron?'

Cathy looked completely blank, as though he had asked her what she thought of global warming or the war in Bosnia, or anything else on which she had never been tested by anyone of her acquaintance.

Fergus was backing Nick's question by staring a hard challenge at her.

'He seems very nice,' she said, glancing at Fergus at the same time. 'You know him better than I do.' Even when she lied she had to qualify it with a get-out clause.

'I like him,' Fergus said, making a point of his openness in doing so. 'He has a good face.'

'That's all right then,' Cathy said. She was bristling because they had cornered her.

Nick said, 'I'm serious, Cathy. I want your support on this one. He isn't like any of the others. He's a good man and he loves me, and if my friends can't accept that, they'll just have to stay out of our lives until we've proved them wrong.'

'Fine,' she said.

'Not fine. I want you to be part of it. I want the two of you to get on with each other. Just try, for my sake.'

'Fine,' she repeated, and Nick knew that he would get no more out of her. It wasn't until he and Aaron were walking home together, at the end of the evening, after everyone else had gone to Tito's, that he began to be angry.

'Who the fuck does she think she is anyway?' he sputtered.

'Who?' Aaron was surprised by the suddenness of Nick's outburst. Only a moment before they had been walking in what he had taken to be harmonious, moonlit companionship.

'Cathy,' Nick spat the name. 'Who d'you think? She always does this, and she always gets away with it. Not this time. It's my life and I'll fall in love with whoever the fuck I want.'

'She doesn't approve of me?' Aaron tried to make the question sound like a rational enquiry.

'It's nothing to do with you. The sour bitch just can't stand to see anyone happy.'

'I thought she was your best friend. She's probably just worried about you. I expect she's being cautious, like any good friend would. That's natural.'

'She's no right to be cautious. Who does she think paid for her fucking holiday anyway? Ungrateful bitch.'

'Did you?' It was the first time Aaron had heard it mentioned that anyone was being paid for.

'Don't,' Nick said. 'Don't get me started on that. When I think of all I've done for her over the years.'

Nick looked at Aaron and saw the alarm in his features, and realised that he had been shouting. Aaron was walking a little further apart from him than a lover might. By way of mitigation, Nick said, 'It isn't your fault.'

'Maybe you shouldn't be shouting at me then.'

'It had to come out somehow.' Nick, deciding that was explanation and apology enough, changed the subject. 'I'll be glad to be home and get some proper food. I'm sick of all this Indian stuff.'

'You never eat Indian food.' Aaron spoke in a tone of flat contradiction, the need to expose an untruth outweighing any sense of tact.

'Yes I do. What was that thing I had tonight? It wasn't proper food. It wasn't pizza or burger or anything that normal people eat.'

'It wasn't Indian either. It was tourist food.'

'Whatever it was, it was disgusting. There's nothing wrong with a good curry, if you're pissed enough, but not every day.'

'Most days,' Aaron said, 'you eat fish and chips.'

'But they're not like the ones you get at home, are they? Anyway, you can't talk. You ate nothing.'

'I couldn't. Big emotion always gets me in the stomach.'

'What's that supposed to mean?'

'Nothing. Being off your food is a traditional symptom of being in love, I suppose.'

Flattered, Nick rose above the squabbling atmosphere between them, and he linked his arm in Aaron's. If he were loved that much, it didn't matter what anyone thought, not even Cathy.

'Andrew seems nice,' Aaron said, looking for a neutral remark with which to clear the air.

'Do you think so?' It was Nick's turn to be taken aback, since his opinion was one which he had received directly from Cathy. 'He hasn't got much going on up top, and he's as wet as a weekend in Wales. I don't know what you find to talk to him about.'

'A lot. He's a bit worried at the moment. Fergus has said that he wants their relationship to end when they get back.'

'He does, does he?' If it was that official, Nick could understand why Fergus had been in such a state. 'That's no surprise. We've all been expecting that for a long time.'

'Andrew wasn't. He was only saying yesterday that this holiday had brought them closer than they've ever been. He's in a bad way now. He doesn't think that he could live without Fergus.'

'Everyone thinks that.' There was a note of brutality in Nick's pragmatism.

Aaron's arm tensed a little. In a voice which sounded afraid of the words it was uttering, he said, 'And what if I came to feel the same way about you?'

'You're different,' Nick said. 'We're different.' Nick tugged on Aaron's arm to stop him walking, reached up and pulled the lofty head down towards his own. 'You're not going to have to live without me. We're going to stay together, no matter how bad things get. I won't let you go.'

Nick thought that that should have been a big romantic moment, but Aaron drew back, the moon on his face and his eyebrows knitted with worry, and he asked, 'Why should things get bad?'

'They always do.'

'I thought this was supposed to be different.'

Nick let out a breath of impatience. 'Everyone has their ups and downs. We've got to be realistic. This is a holiday, not real life. I've been in enough relationships to know what the pitfalls are. But nothing is going to break us up, if we work at it.'

'You're right,' Aaron said. 'I suppose. It just seems a

bit bleak. I've always thought that life should be more pleasurable than anything.'

'Stick with me,' Nick said.

By this time they were walking again, getting near Aaron's hotel, in the warm air and to the sounds of insects and dogs and the occasional, distant suggestion of music from the direction of the beach. The heat of the other's hand in his made each man feel powerful, as though, with a man such as this to live for, he could do anything.

Aaron said, 'I love you,' but softly, as though the words were new to him and he had just that minute grasped their meaning.

Any opera freak will tell you that the combination of life-threatening illness and infatuation is an inflammatory one. More so, if the attachment is less than a week old and neither of the attached has yet allowed their halos to slip. There are few sensations more gratifying than being indispensible, and few creatures who provoke indispensibility more than a complete and incontinent invalid. The patient, too, is gratified, if the attention he receives is faultless, since he will undergo an experience he has not known since infancy, and he is bound to mistake his fevered gratitude and his nurse's overwhelming solicitude for the symptoms of a love of mythical proportions. At the onset of any entanglement the boundaries are tenuous, formed by pleasure and attraction. The infliction of something nasty on one of the protagonists serves as a short cut to more mature parameters, of duty and suffering and self-denial and the tolerance of nauseating smells, and all the other proofs of durable affection. Mistaking a dramatic illness for the worst that can happen, the lovers conclude that their relationship has been tried and tested, and they emerge with an idealistic notion of their own fortitude.

Nick felt the first twinge in his bowels at twelve minutes past six on the morning after he had wolfed down the calamari and bacteria stir-fry, when he managed to wake

Aaron with a groan of uninhibited eloquence. There are some who would advocate the stoic approach in such circumstances, but Nick, in this instance anyway, decided to start as he meant to go on, and thought it best to produce a noise which had the ring of an emergency to it.

A feeling of vague unease had intruded on his sleep, but he was not someone who was inclined to open his eyes with a start and see what the matter was. He had learned, from experience, a sequence of mental exercises which made the attainment of consciousness less of a trial. The first was to remember where he was and the second to remember how he had got there. The third, and often the most taxing, was to remember the identity of the man sleeping beside him. That done, one eye could be prised open until it showed a gap the thickness of a sheet of paper, so that he could see how the land lay and whether or not it was advisable to seem to be awake.

Aaron's hotel room was a space of such porridge-coloured anonymity that Nick's first befuddled reaction that morning was to think how easily it could be transformed into something tolerable by a few judiciously hung swags of the right kind of cotton. He was deciding the exact shade of yellow required when an involuntary contraction, too close to the sphincter for comfort, persuaded him that there were more urgent considerations than environmental oversensitivity. An attempt at movement produced the twinge, which was more of a sharp stab if he thought about it, and that resulted in the groan. Aaron sat up in bed as though a glass of chilled lager had been poured down the back of his neck.

'What?' he said, looking about him, as though the groan could have come from inside the dun and brown plastic wardrobe.

A drawn out and heart-rending 'Uh,' seemed the most appropriate and effective response, from a brain which had not yet located that part of its structure responsible for polysyllabic utterance. Nick then proceeded to fill in the details with a bubbling at the corner of his mouth, and a fart which somehow conveyed a disquieting impression of liquidity. He was not so much sweating as percolating, at a rate which made him wonder if he wouldn't die of drowning before dehydration got to him. He looked at his hand across the pillow, and saw that the skin was the colour and texture of the flesh of a cooked mullet.

'This,' Nick thought, 'has a bit of mileage in it.' Only then did he remember that he was in India, and that death was not an unlikely prospect.

'Are you sick?' Aaron asked.

'Did Rose Kennedy have a fucking black frock? What do I have to do? Ooze pus from my earholes?' Having rediscovered the power of speech, Nick reinforced his response with a little illustrative retching.

Aaron rolled him over to ascertain the exact state of things below. As he might have suspected, there had been a certain amount of leakage. There was a rich and unappetising smell. With words of tactful encouragement, in a voice not yet entirely devoid of sleep, Aaron half-carried Nick to the bathroom. Fortunately, it being a westernised hotel, there were what are known as en suite facilities. Once Nick had been placed on the lavatory, Aaron would have left him there, saying that he had to deal with the bed, but Nick held on to his hand with the grip of the desperate.

'Don't go,' Nick said. 'Don't leave me alone. Help me. I think I'm going to die.' As the last word was spoken, vomit surged through his mouth. Most of it landed on his knees.

The shock of being sprayed with sick brought Aaron completely to his senses and, fully awake and remembering the degree to which he was in love, he said, 'I'm not going anywhere. Of course not. You're not going to die.'

'I am,' Nick howled.

Aaron bent over and kissed him, more, perhaps, at that

point, as a gesture of good faith than as a mark of affection. Nick sniffed. Exploding sounds came from beneath him, as though someone had let off a two hundred rupee firecracker in the lavatory bowl. As if he were not exuding enough substances already, snot and tears began to flood down his face, caused partly by discomfort, more by fear and shame.

Nick could see no further than two possibilities. The first was a painful death, and the second was that Aaron would be so disgusted that their relationship would end. Searching Aaron's face for signs of this revulsion, he found only concern. That was the moment when he realised that Aaron's goodness ran deep, and it was also the moment when Nick began to be afraid of him.

When the worst seemed to be over, Aaron stood Nick in the shower, supporting him with one arm while he hosed both of them down, soaping the insides of Nick's legs with a detached gentleness. Aaron's equanimity astonished Nick, whose own reactions to bodily functions had always been on the squeamish side. The sight of vomit on a pavement had always made him feel sick, and he was one of those people who had to leave the room if a baby needed changing. He'd been pleased by the widespread introduction of condoms, when he discovered that it meant the unpleasantness could be flung to the side of the bed, leaving a dick tainted with nothing more than the faint odour of rubber. Once, he had finished an otherwise promising relationship after discovering skidmarks in the man's underwear, a phenomenon he had always been careful to conceal in his own. He knew that he could never have done for Aaron what Aaron was now doing for him.

Aaron dried him and wrapped him in a beach towel, and read the medical notes in the back of his traveller's diary, to find out the difference between amoebic and bacillary dysentery. Once he had established that there was cause for serious concern, he dressed and made his way down to reception, to lobby for clean sheets and the services of a doctor.

Aaron almost gave the impression that he was enjoying himself during the days which followed. He fretted a bit, naturally, and he had to avert his eyes while Nick was having his twice-daily injections. Otherwise, he managed to pad out his nursing role with small pleasures and minor outlets for competence. He hired a bicycle and went backwards and forwards between the hotel and Calingute for visits to the chemist and laundry; he mopped Nick's brow and mixed the solutions of anti-dehydration salts. During the long bouts of feverish sleep he sat close by, on the small balcony, with one eye on a paperback lent to him by Andrew, and the other eye on Nick. He slept, like a new mother, ready to waken and investigate at the smallest hint of alarm. He marked, with satisfaction, the progress away from danger: the first sip that could be taken without retching, the first unhurried removal from bed to lavatory.

Several times he went over to the Gregory Garden to fetch things that Nick needed, and always he would search out Cathy, and elicit the promise of a visit, which she somehow never got around to fulfilling.

'She keeps herself busy,' Nick said. 'Sickness isn't really her kind of thing.'

At other times Nick railed against her. 'The bitch. When you think of all I've done for her and she couldn't pay me one lousy visit. I might be dead for all she cares. You soon find out who your friends are. If that's the way she feels then she can pay me back all the fucking money she owes me for her fucking holiday. This is what you get for being nice to people. Well that's it. It's just you and me from now on. I don't see why I should care about anyone who doesn't care about me.'

Aaron tried to be soothing. 'Don't say things like that.

You'll upset yourself. I expect it's my fault. She doesn't like me very much.'

'What makes you say that?'

'It's just an impression I got.' Aaron showed signs of unease as he answered, picking at the ball of his thumb and avoiding Nick's eye.

'She has no business liking or disliking you. I know what she's like. She's afraid that she's going to lose out now that I've got you instead. Well she's right. I won't have anything more to do with her.'

Fergus and Andrew dropped by once, and stood for a few minutes, awkwardly, just inside the doorway. They had been fighting on the way over and their ceasefire was barely maintained for the sickroom.

'That was nice of them,' Aaron said, after they had gone.

'Big fucking deal,' Nick said, and closed his eyes to show that he was too weak to talk about it.

Aaron came and sat on the bed, close by Nick. He might have thought that Nick was asleep because, after a while, he said in a voice that was low enough not to wake him, 'So this is love.'

Nick was not asleep. 'What do you mean?' he asked suspiciously, without opening his eyes.

'I don't know. It's something beyond qualification. You can lose your temper like that and I still love you. I was even looking at the zits on your arse the other day and thinking how much I loved you. And you have very thin eyelashes. Did you know that? I always thought, before, that there was something sinister about that, to have eyelids like a reptile, but on you I think it's beautiful. Even if you told me you were a murderer now, I'd love you no less. All this is out of my hands, as though I loved you before I ever saw you, and it's only now that life makes any sense. You've saved me, you know that? I don't know from what, but you've saved me from it. Perhaps I do know what it is, because the worst thing I can think of now is a life without you, and you've saved me from that.' Aaron's voice had deepened and slowed as he spoke and, as the words progressed, it sounded as if each syllable was causing him discomfort.

'I don't know,' Nick said, 'what you see in me.'

The delirium came and went for the first few days. In the bad times Nick would be aware of nothing more than the turning of the relentless ceiling fan, or the colour of the box in which the doctor kept his syringes, which was a sort of scuffed yellow. The pain could be unremitting, blurring all sense of time and reality. He had conversations with people who were not there, and would have no idea afterwards whether he had spoken aloud and been heard by Aaron, or whether all the talk had been in his head and dreams. Once, he thought he was in hell, and the voice said, 'Oh good, you're home.'

In an apparently lucid moment he asked if Aaron knew how to 'do astral flying'. Without waiting for an answer, he went on, 'We could go flying together. That'd be the best.' Because Aaron failed to think of a response to that, he never found out whether it was a serious or a delirious suggestion.

In some of the better times, Nick felt compelled to talk about the distant past; about his mother and what a game girl she had been, with her trysts down the docks and the arrangement with the policeman next-door who, when Nick was eleven, was the first person he had sex with. Nick said that he and his mother were very close and told how, even as a child, he used to keep her company with her bottle of Bacardi of an evening. By the time he was ten they'd have a bottle each. His father had disappeared soon after his birth, because of the lack of family resemblance between them, a discrepancy which had the Methodist congregation surmising what his father had already suspected. He said that he escaped home himself at the age of fourteen, and he was frank with his tales of working with the only assets he had. He told Aaron that he wasn't proud of having been a whore, but that he had come to accept it; that he had known what he was doing.

'But you were a child,' Aaron said. 'It must have had some effect.'

Nick was used to hearing that kind of amateur psychology. He said that he was very advanced for his age; that he was used to being fucked by old men anyway and didn't see why he shouldn't be paid for it. 'You have to laugh about it. The things that some of them wanted to get up to. There was one old fart who was a real sugar daddy. He used to buy us presents. He always had two of us. The other boy, I forget what his name was, was chained to the end of the bed and had to watch us and bark like a dog. I'd be strapped up so I couldn't move a muscle, with a leather mask that covered my face, and a compartment over the nose for a rag soaked in poppers. I'd be so off my head I couldn't tell if I was being fucked or not. You couldn't scream anyway with the mask being so tight. He was all right really, that bloke. He'd be all sorry afterwards and we could make him buy us anything. I knew what I was doing.'

As he spoke, Nick saw Aaron cry for the first time. Aaron lay on his back, expressionless and a bit pale, and tears dripped onto the pillow on either side of his head. Nick asked him what the matter was.

'I don't like it,' he said. 'I don't like the idea of someone doing that to you.'

Nick said that he had been there of his own free will.

'You were a child,' Aaron said.

Nick said that he wasn't bothered by it. 'It's not a bad thing,' he said, 'to give over control sometimes, to lie there and be fucked and abused and treated like a piece of meat. Sometimes you need it. It satisfies something. I don't want you to go thinking that I'm soiled goods. I'm not falling into that little game. I'm sorry now that I told you about it.'

'No one,' Aaron said, 'is ever going to do anything like that to you again.'

For Nick, that had the ring of a commitment, and he felt as though he were home and dry. One of those embraces which are as comfortable as sleep followed, and Nick told Aaron that he felt safe with him.

Aaron came back from Calingute and saw what he took to be a remarkable improvement in Nick's condition. He was sitting up in bed, dry and smiling. On the bedside table there was a glass and a whisky bottle which was two-thirds full. Nick had called room service.

'Was that wise?' Aaron asked.

'What?'

'Should you be drinking with all those drugs inside you?'

'I always drink when I'm on drugs,' Nick said, laughing. He saw, from Aaron's expression, that a cavalier attitude was getting him nowhere. He tried another tack. 'It's the only thing I can keep down. I thought of it while you were out and it seemed worth a try. The doctor said I had to drink something. So far, so good. It's whisky or dehydration, I'm afraid.'

It was obvious that Aaron wasn't entirely convinced, so Nick caught him by the belt loops of his trousers and pulled him towards the bed. 'Come here, you gorgeous man,' he said. He noticed that Aaron had an erection before he even had a chance to get him unzipped. 'I think I'm well enough for this now,' Nick said, and pushed his mouth all the way down over Aaron's dick to show what he could take without gagging.

Aaron was so overwrought after the days of abstinence that he pinned Nick to the bed and fucked his mouth as hard and fast as he thought he could get away with. When Nick smothered and spluttered he tried to pull out, but Nick caught him by the arse and rammed him back in again, thinking that it was worth it for the whisky. In the strange way that these things happen, Nick reached a point where he realised that he was enjoying it, and that Aaron couldn't be rough enough, and that he wanted the dick to choke him. After Aaron had come, Nick shoved his face into him until breathing was impossible and, when he was on the point of blacking out, shot spunk halfway up Aaron's spine.

Nick dozed that afternoon without delirious shouting and was in restlessly good spirits by the evening. He would have liked to go out, but his legs were so weak that they buckled when he tried to stand.

'I'm bored,' he said. 'I want visitors. I want to go back to the Gregory Garden and sit on the veranda with my friends. I hate this room. If I'm just going to be sitting around anyway I might as well be doing it there.'

'Maybe tomorrow,' Aaron said. 'I'll get a rickshaw. You're obviously better.' He was uneasy, picking things up and taking them across the room and putting them down elsewhere, with no apparent reason. Sometimes he would look at Nick and breathe in a little, as though he were about to say something, then stop himself and find some other object to transport.

'Stop it,' Nick said. 'You're getting on my tits. Haven't you got a book to read or something?'

'Is it always like that?' Aaron spoke with an agonised hesitancy which was supposed to indicate what he was talking about.

'Is what?'

'Sex.'

'Like what?'

'Nothing,' Aaron said. 'Never mind.'

A little later, with no preamble, Aaron said, 'Are you going to tell me your secrets now?'

Nick flinched. 'What secrets? I've told you everything.'

Aaron said, 'Oh,' and it seemed as if he might drop it there, but half a minute later he was sitting on the bed and looking earnest, and saying, 'All that stuff you were going on about yesterday. You told me you had secrets. Things you were ashamed of and never told. You said you wanted to tell me. You said it was disgusting and I was the only person who would understand.'

'Did I?'

'Yes.' Aaron couldn't understand why Nick was behaving as though a trap were being laid for him.

Nick shrugged, as casually as he could manage. 'I don't know what I could have been talking about, unless it was all that stuff about being on the game when I was a teenager.'

'And being encased from head to toe in rubber while you were fucked by coachloads of elderly paedophiles. No, you'd told me all that already. You know you had. This was something else. Something that's really bugging you.'

'Nope,' Nick said. 'Sorry. Means nothing to me. I must have been delirious.'

But later, when Nick was very drunk and out of control, and pressing himself against Aaron like a child who doesn't want to be left at school, he said, 'Don't ask me about all that stuff yet. I will tell you, someday, but give me time.'

Aaron made noises of comfort, and stroked Nick's head until he was sleeping. Though he had doubts about Nick by then, he felt that it would have been churlish to admit them.

Even by his own standards, Nick drank a lot during those last days in Goa. At first, while he was recovering from his illness and incapable of going much further than the veranda, the amount was not noticeable. Aaron was happy to see him getting better, and content to spend a few days sitting with him while they drank beer and talked about the future. It was not until Aaron noticed that he had a hangover for the third morning in a row that he began to consider how much alcohol they were consuming in the course of a day. He decided to lay off the booze for a bit. When they ordered breakfast that morning and Nick asked for his usual, Aaron said that he wanted plain pineapple juice.

'No rum?' asked Anthony, in his tone of mocking surprise.

Nick asked if there was something the matter.

'No,' Aaron said. 'I just thought I'd give it a rest for a bit.'

'Suit yourself,' Nick said.

'Do you normally drink this much?' Aaron asked.

'What do you mean, this much? I don't drink any more than you do.'

'I know,' Aaron admitted. 'I just thought we were over-doing it a bit.'

'It's supposed to be a frigging holiday. Stop being such a

bloody granny. I'm trying to have a nice time. It's not my fault I got ill and I'm too fucking weak to do anything but sit here. I'm trying to make the best of things. Just because you've decided to go on the wagon there's no need to get on your high horse and spoil my fun.'

'Sorry,' Aaron said. 'I was only asking.' He was feeling a bit cowed by Nick's fierceness.

'Sup up or shut up, that's what I say.' Nick was addressing not only Aaron, but Fergus, who was coming up the steps at that moment, with a joint inverted in the cup of his hand which, glancing around him, he made to pass to Aaron. Anthony didn't approve of his guests smoking in full view of the road.

'No thanks,' Aaron said. 'I'm getting a bit bored with being stoned all the time.'

'Ignore him,' Nick said, taking the joint for himself. 'He's being a real little priss this morning for some reason.'

'I'm not. I just thought that I'd start not smoking until the evening, and have a few hours a day of not being a zombie.'

'For shit's sake boys,' Fergus said wearily. 'Don't you two start. I get enough of this bickering at home.'

Aaron felt that he and Nick had been behaving badly, and was ashamed. Nick, on the other hand, giggled. 'We're like an old married couple already,' he said. He reached across and gave Aaron's hand a squeeze.

'Anjuna day today,' Fergus said. 'You two going?'

Aaron said that he'd like to, if Nick was feeling well enough.

'I've been,' Nick said, in a bothered voice. 'It's just a lot of old hippies buying tat.'

Fergus said that Aaron should see it once, and Nick agreed, but said that he didn't think he was up to it himself. There was no reason why that should stop Aaron going.

'I don't know,' Aaron said. At the suggestion of spending a

day apart from Nick he was seized with a mild kind of panic. There was no rational explanation that he could think of for this, except that they had so few days left before Nick would go home and he continue his journey round the world, that he felt they should make the most of every moment they could have in each other's company now. 'Maybe we could just spend the day on the beach instead.'

'Maybe,' Nick said, so doubtfully and pulling such a face that it didn't seem very likely.

Aaron found he was feeling a little cross with Nick, but told himself that he was being unreasonable. It wasn't as though Nick had decided to be ill. He thought about how Fergus had just caught them out bickering, and decided that going to Anjuna on his own would be better than hanging around on the veranda and blaming Nick for his boredom. 'I'll go,' he said. 'Will you be all right? You don't mind?'

'No, no, you go. Enjoy yourself. Don't worry about me.' Nick diluted his attempt at martyrdom by adding, 'Bring me back something nice. Expensive nice, mind. None of that old rubbish the crusties go for.'

To begin with, Aaron thought that he was enjoying himself at the market. It was larger and more colourful than he had expected. There were, as Nick had said, a lot of old hippies buying tat, but there was a lot more besides. There were old hippies selling tat to support themselves through the rainy season, and wannabe hippies with their new piercings and tattoos who were just there for the winter before going back to their computer terminals in the West. All the traders had come in from down the coast and the pastel package-tourists had been bussed up, to buy their token tie-dye waistcoat and wonder why the men selling the King-Size Rizzlas were doing such a roaring trade at eighty rupees a packet.

Aaron was in an odd frame of mind and, having been round the whole market once, he sat down at the cafe to think. On one level he was ecstatically happy because he was in love. On another level he was impatient to get on to the next stage, to be home again and busy and making a new life with Nick. It occurred to him that this was rushing things a little, but he told himself that he and Nick still had the interregnum while he continued his travels. Then he worried about that, and couldn't help wondering whether Nick would lose interest in him during his absence. There was no question, they had decided, but that each of them should go ahead with his immediate plans. This they called being sensible and not losing their heads over one another. Nick had sworn to him that he was monogamous by nature and that, once he was in love and in a relationship, there was no possibility of him sleeping with another man. Aaron had made the same assurance. They had decided that the period apart would be a way of founding their union in trust. Not being an idiot, Aaron recognised that you had to know someone before you could trust him, and he had to admit that, however much he was in love, he did not know Nick. In the meantime, however, he had his instincts to follow. Aaron was one of those fortunate creatures who had never once been let down by intuition, or so, in his unassailable self-confidence, he thought. He trusted instinct completely, and it told him that Nick was genuine.

All the way round the market he had been thinking about Nick in relation to everything he saw. Now, thinking about Nick more specifically was making him maudlin. He decided that he would go back to Baga as soon as he had found the right present. He became so anxious about what to buy that the purchase took several hours of ransacking the displays of every Tibetan and Kashmiri at Anjuna. He chose, eventually, an overpriced wooden Ganesh which probably wasn't as old as it looked, and set out over the cliffs with his token wrapped in newspaper and string. It was the hot part of the afternoon and sweat poured off him, but he walked and scrambled as fast as he could manage, worrying obsessively that he had chosen badly and bought something that Nick wouldn't like. No part of his brain was available to speculate on whether an apparently intelligent man shouldn't have better things to think about.

So pleased was he at the reunion that he wouldn't have noticed or cared if Nick was standing on his head with drunkenness but, as it was, Nick had gone to bed for the afternoon, glad to be able to have a few hours' sleep without an erection poking in his back. Aaron, seeing his relative sobriety and remembering that he had asked a question that morning which had been tantamount to an accusation, was overcome with guilt.

'I missed you,' he said. 'I'm sorry, about this morning. I don't know why I was so ratty. I'd rather do nothing with you than do anything else on my own.'

In a magnanimous tone, Nick said, 'You do get yourself worked up about things when there's no need.'

'I know. I want everything to be perfect, that's all.'

'Well, we won't have any more nonsense about drinking then. It was like having breakfast with the Salvation Army. What did you get? Is that a present?'.

'I don't know if you'll like it.'

Nick pulled the paper off and looked at the carving for a long time. 'What is it?' he asked.

'It's Ganesh. His father cut his head off and gave him an elephant's head instead. He's supposed to be lucky.'

'He's got a bit of a pot belly.'

'You don't like it?'

'I expect it'll grow on me. It's not the sort of thing I would have bought myself.' Then, because Aaron looked so crestfallen, he propped the Ganesh against the wall and stood back and looked at it some more, and said that he loved it and it was perfect.

They went on from there with the best of intentions. They would lie in bed in the mornings and plan the day, maybe deciding to go to Mapsa after breakfast and spend the afternoon on the beach. Nick would get a buzz out of seeing Aaron's excitement at the prospect of such simple things. Then Aaron would start to kiss him and he'd say, 'Wait a second. I haven't brushed my teeth.' To which Aaron would reply that he didn't mind, but get the impression that his breath stank and go to the basin to do something about it. Once Aaron was out of bed, Nick would say, 'Skin up for me, sweetheart. There's a fresh tola in the silver box.' Aaron would comment, but not necessarily with any reproach, that it was a bit early for that sort of thing, before rolling the joint anyway. Any attempt he made at seduction after that would be countered by Nick saying that he was too stoned to have sex.

Not that they never did it at all, but Nick considered Aaron to be completely oversexed. Aaron, who only had to look at Nick's face to get an erection, was forced to agree that his demands might seem unreasonable. As often as not, when they did anything, Nick would make a show of generous acquiescence. He'd roll over on his stomach and say, 'Come on then, if you must do something. Jerk off over my arse.'

Though he would not have admitted it, Nick was confused by this state of affairs. He had always considered his libido to be a match for anyone's, and here he was, in love and with a man whom he honestly considered to be the most sexually exciting creature on the planet, yet apparently incapable of doing anything about it. As soon as he was alone for a few minutes he would masturbate, usually with some vision of Aaron in his mind. Some days this happened two or three times. Then, in reality, Aaron would be naked beside him in bed, erect and desperate to love, and nothing would happen. Nick's fantasies were usually of a violent nature – of being tied in some humiliating position while Aaron fucked and abused him, came in his face and walked away without a word, leaving him whimpering and helpless – while in real life Aaron was gentle and tactile and there was a lot of eye contact. Privately, Nick was certain that the matter would resolve itself in time. Meanwhile he took the moral high ground, and kept Aaron in his place by accusing him of being a sex pest who just wanted to dump his sperm on the nearest available surface.

From the beginning, they had dealt openly with the fucking thing. Neither of them was very enamoured of the butch and bitch syndrome, and both of them said that they weren't that keen on being fucked either. Nick, who had the greater sexual experience, said that there was nothing to worry about. He had been in relationships before where both parties had felt the same way. It was a question of trust, he said. If you were in love with someone, being fucked by him was an act of generosity on your part. It might be painful at first, but the pleasure you were giving to the other would turn you on. He could be, he said, like a bitch on heat in those circumstances. Aaron said that he would give it a try. Nick fucked him a couple of times before they left Goa, and it seemed as though Aaron might get used to it.

Once, Nick thought he was ready for the reciprocation.

It was a day when Aaron had been having his own way in general. They'd decided to spend the morning on the beach, but Nick got talking to a couple of people at breakfast, and Cathy was on form and being very funny and they had a couple of drinks and suddenly it was lunchtime, so Nick thought it seemed sensible to stay on the veranda and order some food. Aaron had been silent and restless, and when Nick asked him to go down to the room to get a fresh packet of skins, he glared and snapped, 'Go yourself. You're not an invalid now.'

'All right,' Nick said. 'Keep your hair on. I was only asking.'

Aaron followed Nick down to the room. When they were alone, Nick turned on him and asked, 'What the fuck did you think you were doing, embarrassing me in front of my friends?'

'I thought we were going to the beach.' Aaron was tight-lipped, as though he had finally got to use a sentence which had been long simmering in his brain.

'We are.'

'When?'

'When I've bloody finished my drink.'

'You've had since eight o'clock this morning to finish your drink. You haven't left the compound for four days. If you don't want to go, say so. If you do, we're going now.'

'You go then. I'll follow you.'

'No. We're going now.'

'All right,' Nick said. 'All right. We're going to the beach. Anything to stop you shouting at me.'

What frightened Nick into submission was that Aaron was not shouting at all. He spoke in the quiet, calm and determined voice of someone who knows exactly what he has to say, and exactly what he will do if things don't go his way. Nick decided that the wisest course of action would be not to test his patience.

Though he grizzled a lot about being inadequate among all the tans and muscles, Nick quite enjoyed himself once they were out in the sun, waving away the fruit ladies. He said, petulantly, that he didn't know what Aaron was doing with a fat old frump like him. Instead of the usual crooning reassurance, Aaron gave him a withering once-over and said flatly, 'You're fine. I like you the way you are.'

Nick said that he loved it when Aaron was being masterful. Though he used the cliché facetiously, there was a level on which he meant it. He preferred Aaron to treat him this way. It wasn't as disconcerting as all the usual love and concern and goodness.

It might have been the harsh treatment, or just the sun on his back, or maybe it was watching tattooed men play beach tennis in next to nothing, or possibly the sight of Aaron, prone and covered in oil with his heavy dick hardly concealed to the public; most probably it was the combination that made Nick nearly breathless with lust that afternoon.

'Aaron?' he said, in a whisper, close by his ear.

'What?'

'I want you to fuck me when we get back.'

Aaron had to turn on his stomach immediately to hide his reaction to the proposal. 'Do you mean it?'

'I'm squirming for it.' Nick's voice carried a rumble of sexual hunger.

They didn't stay much longer on the beach, each of them distracted by the prospect of consummation. Aaron's hotel was the nearest, so they went there, hardly able to look at one another and carrying their possessions in front of them for decency. They ran up the stairs and Aaron had so much trouble unlocking the door that he began to think he had got the rooms mixed up. They gorged on each other's faces while they pulled off the few clothes they were wearing, and then Nick fell back on the bed and Aaron pushed his knees up to his ears and looked at his arse like a dog at a butcher's window.

'Tie me up,' Nick said, hoarse with frustration that he should need to ask.

That put Aaron off-balance for a second, but he was so desperate that he would have done anything he was asked. He looked about him for possible restraints and came up with a belt and a pillowcase and the sleeves of a shirt. Within a minute Nick was trussed, and he heard the tearing of a condom wrapper behind him and felt the cold slab of lube being pushed against his sphincter.

Something went wrong. Aaron was only halfway in and it hurt more than anything Nick had ever known; like hot skewers, like slamming a thumb in a door jamb. He screamed.

'What is it?' Aaron asked, pulling out and cradling Nick's head and untying him all at once.

'I can't. I want to, but I can't. I'm sorry.' Nick could hardly speak in the ebbing pain.

Aaron said that it didn't matter.

'Your dick's too big,' Nick said, knowing that he had taken bigger in his time and that was not the problem, but at least it was flattering. 'We can try another time. Maybe when I'm stoned and we've got some poppers.'

Aaron said that it didn't matter.

Nick said, 'We just have to be patient. It's not easy for me.'

Aaron said that it was his fault. His face was white with guilt.

'No,' Nick said. 'Come on. I love you.'

'Maybe that's what it is,' Aaron said.

Nick salvaged what he could of the lust by making Aaron stand over him and jerk off in his face. He put Aaron's foot on his chest and watched as Aaron lost control of himself. That seemed fine, when Aaron was no more than a pornographic image, towering over him. Nick got excited again, and came as Aaron's spunk came flying towards his open mouth.

Aaron asked him if he wanted to talk about it, and Nick asked him what he meant, in a tone which indicated that he'd rather forget the whole thing.

'Maybe,' Aaron said, 'it's because of all the things that happened to you.'

'What things?'

'When you were on the game and stuff, and being fucked by the man next door when you were eleven.'

'So what?'

'So maybe you associate being fucked with being abused, and maybe you can't take it from someone who loves you.'

That sounded a bit simplistic to Nick, and he was about to tell Aaron that he'd been fucked by plenty of people who loved him, but then he realised that it would only make things worse, so he said, 'Maybe.'

Aaron, counting that as progress, seemed happier. He said that they had all the time in the world to sort things out. He asked Nick if he trusted him.

'You're the perfect man,' Nick said.

That was one of the times when Aaron let Nick fuck him. He was high on emotion and Nick made the most of it.

At the back of his mind, Nick couldn't help but be cynical. The whole thing seemed too good to be true. Like most people, he'd spent a lot of time looking for and dreaming of the perfect lover. One way or another, they had all turned out to be shits. Aaron had all the appearances of perfection and all the appearances of loving him without question. It was impossible to believe that there wasn't a flaw in him somewhere: it wasn't in his body or his dick, or his kindness or tolerance or generosity or intelligence. Until he found the flaw, Nick wasn't inclined to give Aaron the benefit of the doubt. He'd been around too much for that.

And this was still a holiday romance. Despite all the promises and all their talk of a future with one another, there was still no guarantee that anything would last beyond Goa; that, once they were home and out of the sunshine, Aaron would see Nick for what he really was and realise that their lives would never fit together. Aaron had described his house to Nick: the quiet street, the stainless steel kitchen, the dinner parties he cooked for his friends and who they were. Names that were not exactly famous in themselves, but known; people who had done things. Once, when someone had brought a Sunday paper out from home, Aaron leafed through it, saying things like, 'Oh good. Ursula got her piece in at last. She sweated blood over that one.' Or, 'I wish they'd stop printing all this crap about Kenneth. He's very nice really.' There were references in his conversation to his publicist, and to being tired of parties where people just stood around talking about books until the champagne ran out.

Nick knew he was afraid of Aaron's life. Aaron was the one who was free to cross boundaries. He could, without compromising himself, slum it with Nick and his friends. He could take drugs and go to nightclubs and gossip mindlessly about characters from soap operas, and the next day be back among his own kind, making his trip to the inferno no more than a titillating anecdote of life on the other side. It was all very well for them to congratulate themselves on how much they had in common, in a place where there was little to do but consume hash by the tola and watch the sun set, but what was Nick going to talk about at Aaron's highbrow gatherings? Anne Rice? That, at least, was the way Nick saw it, though, for the moment, he wasn't going to say so.

The day approached when Nick would fly west and Aaron continue east. Nick would say how happy he was and that he never wanted to go back. They could stay and make a life in Goa.

As if Aaron had considered the possibility himself, he would tell Nick that he wouldn't like Goa in the rainy season, or in the hot, and Nick would agree that it was a silly idea, and abandon the fantasy, resigning himself to the months ahead, of waiting for Aaron while he played out the rest of his journey. When Nick thought about Aaron in the places he might go through, in Tokyo and Sydney and San Francisco and New York, all he could see was an image of him surrounded by men who were more beautiful than the man he was supposed to be faithful to. Younger, slimmer, brainier, richer men with worthwhile lives to offer; bubble-arsed men who could be fucked easily and would be glad to be fucked by a man like Aaron.

Sounding desperate, Nick would promise Aaron again and again that he wasn't even going to look for another man while he waited for him.

Sometimes all the fear would petrify into the self-preserving thought that if Aaron never came back to him, they had had the best of their times already. Life could never be one long holiday.

On the penultimate night everyone had supper together at Casa Costanza. Fergus and Andrew were flying out the next afternoon, so it was a kind of last supper. There were thirteen of them altogether, including someone new, called Jason. He was an American whom Cathy had met at Tito's.

It was not, after all, a remarkable meal, except that it gave the impression of lasting two and a half hours longer than it did. Cathy, under an injunction from Nick not to say anything offensive to Aaron, said little at all. Fergus, who had told Andrew that he wanted their relationship to end as soon as the plane landed, held a salt cellar in an adamantine stare for the duration. Andrew not only failed to eat anything that was put in front of him, but rendered it inedible for anyone else by larding it with silent tears. Of the others, two had eaten opium and were wearing beautiful, if inappropriate smiles; one had taken mushroom extract and was holding a hilarious discourse with the lightbulb; and one, who had just decided to become a Sanyatin, was petrifying what conversation there was with the sayings of Oshi. Aside from that the beer was warm and everyone had forgotten to bring skins, except Cathy, who had dropped hers in the river on the way over. The only mechanism which Nick could think of for dealing with the situation was to become astoundingly drunk.

Jason was probably only flirting out of boredom, and Nick was probably only responding to alleviate what was otherwise the dreariest gathering since the last time he had spent Christmas with his mother. Jason, Nick thought, wasn't bad looking. He was a little overgroomed, with capped teeth and hair that took maintenance. His shirt was unbuttoned enough to show a freshly waxed chest. He was telling everyone about a beach masseur he had come across in a secluded place among the rocks, who had sucked him off for an extra fifty rupees.

'What did he look like?' Nick asked, trying to make his interest sound academic, lest Aaron be upset by it.

'Nothing special. An old guy. Any of them'll do it, I'm sure. I mean, bucks really talk around here. I mean, like, sex for less than two dollars, right?'

Aaron said, 'You could have just given him the money, if he was that desperate.'

'Get real,' Jason said, and threw Nick a look of sympathy for being attached to such an invertebrate.

Nick tried to bridge the gap. 'Come on, darling. You'd do the same if you were single. Anyone would.'

Aaron raised an eyebrow at Nick, then returned his attention to Andrew, whom he was making a point of being nice to, in the face of everyone else's indifference.

Jason continued, 'I mean, what's a guy supposed to do round here? It's all couples. Everywhere you look. Goa sucks as far as sex goes.'

Here, he turned his full attention on Nick, with a meaningful glint in his eye.

Nick took that as a compliment. He liked to think he still had pulling power, even if he wasn't on the market. 'You must be very frustrated,' he said.

'Yup. I'm ready for just about anything now.' Jason

glanced at Aaron speculatively, then back at Nick, as if he were double checking them. 'Just about anything at all.'

Nick sat back to take a long drink of beer, and scanned the table to see if anyone else had noticed what was going on. Cathy was the only one who might have picked up on it, but she had just that moment gone for a pee.

'You never know your luck,' Nick said. The meaning of his tone was plain to Jason, but an eavesdropper might have taken it for generalised consolation. 'These things usually happen when you're least expecting them.'

The tide was full out by the time the meal had finished, so they went back along the beach in straggling groups. Aaron pointed out the phosphorescence in the sea and said that he was going to miss the nighttimes most. Nick was drunk and leaning on him a little for support. Ahead of them, Jason and someone else were stripping off for a late swim. Even in the near dark you could tell that he had a fit body.

'Sweetie?' Nick said.

'Yes?'

'Have you ever tried a threesome?'

'No.'

'Do you ever think about it?'

'No. Maybe I used to, but I've never been seriously tempted. It's not my sort of thing. Why are you asking?'

'I just wondered.'

Nick stood behind Aaron with his arms about him. They had stopped walking and were watching the swimmers. Because, though there had been a note of caution in Aaron's voice, there had been no outrage, Nick thought he might press the point.

'What do you think of Jason?' he asked.

'He seems all right. Slightly crass.'

'He's got a nice body, don't you think?'

Aaron turned to face him, breaking his hold. 'What are you saying?' He sounded very sober all of a sudden.

'Nothing. I just thought we might, if you wanted. I wouldn't want you to think you were missing out on anything because of me.'

'I don't believe I'm hearing this.' Aaron sounded in pain.

'I only asked.'

'Is that what you want?'

'We hadn't discussed it. We had to talk about it some-time. Lots of people do it. It wouldn't mean that I loved you less.'

'Is that what you want?' His voice was insistent as he tried to keep emotion out of it and get at the truth.

'No.' Having made his mistake, Nick looked for a way to make the best of it. 'Only if you did. I was trying to find out if you wanted it, to see where we stood. It's the last thing I want, but I probably would have done it for you, if it made you happy. You know I feel guilty because we don't have sex as often as you want. I hate the idea of sleeping with anyone else. I only want you. You know that.' He tried to embrace Aaron, but Aaron slipped through his arms, greased with doubt. 'Look,' Nick said. 'It's over. We've established that it's not what either of us want. Let's forget I ever mentioned it.'

They had one little drama on the day that Aaron left, which Nick said was hardly surprising really, when you considered the trauma of parting.

Because the trains were full and Aaron had to take the only berth available, he was obliged to leave a full two days before Nick was to fly home. Nick woke uncharacteristically early the morning before the sundering, and began to panic about money.

'Sweetie,' he said, as soon as Aaron showed signs of consciousness. 'I suppose I'd better ask Anthony for the bill this morning, so you can see how much you need to change before you settle up with him.'

'Of course,' Aaron said, shamed for not having been the first to mention it. Although he had retained his own hotel room, he had, effectively, been living at the Gregory Garden. It would only be fair to pay half.

The bill came to more than eighteen thousand rupees, which took them by surprise at first, but when they thought about the drinks and cigarettes and meals they had constantly been ordering and putting on the account, it seemed a realistic amount. 'So,' Aaron offered, 'what should I give you? Half?' That, he thought, was being more than generous, since Nick had been outdrinking him at a rate of about three to one, and there had been no suggestion of Nick contributing to the other hotel bill.

'Well, as a matter of fact,' Nick began, 'I'm a bit worried about money. Everyone told me India was going to be dead cheap and I didn't bring nearly enough. I wondered if you could help me out a bit. I'll pay you back when you get home, of course. I hate asking this.'

'Oh for fuck's sake shut up,' Aaron said. 'You don't have to apologise about asking for money. You can have whatever you want. Look, the easiest thing is if I just pay the whole bill.'

As he cycled to the bank in Calingute Aaron did a few calculations. The amount, he decided, was not going to wreck his budget. It might seem a lot by Indian standards, but he could recoup it just by spending a few days less in New York at the end of the trip. Once he was inside the bank he forgot all the mathematics and settled down to enjoy the transaction. He took pleasure in changing pounds to rupees: the tellers in loud nylon saris; the beautiful brass token he was given; the long, inexplicable wait for his number to come up; watching the sweaty impatient tourists who counted their money as suspiciously as if they were engaging in a back alley transaction with a black marketeer. The best part was being given thick bundles of notes bound with heavy staples in exchange for his few, flimsy traveller's cheques. He liked the feeling of wealth as he cycled back with a bag full of cash.

Anthony, when Aaron handed over the bundles, said the whole thing had been unnecessary, that he would have accepted payment in foreign currency. Aaron looked at him, trying to decide how much of his kindness and deference was motivated by self-interest; part of the service demanded by people of an alien culture, whom he probably wouldn't wish to know if it weren't for the fact that they had too much money to spend and he had a family to feed and educate. Then Anthony began to ask him about the other places he might visit, and the curiosity was so disinterested that Aaron decided he had been too cynical: Anthony was probably as nice as he seemed. It was unfortunate that most of the foreigners he came in contact with were too stoned to see him as anything more than a glorified, smiling waiter.

'And Mr Nick?' Anthony asked. 'You will see him again, at home?'

'Oh yes,' Aaron said, and had to walk away while he still had some control over emotions which had been loosened by the unexpected tenderness of Anthony's question.

The last night, though charged with all the feeling that either of them might have expected, was not remarkable in terms of anything that was said or done. Each of them had trouble sleeping.

'Sweetie?' Nick said, when dawn was showing in the cracks between the rooftiles. 'Could I ask you a big favour? I'm still a bit worried about money. I've probably got enough to see me out, but I get so paranoid about being this far from home, if anything went wrong. You couldn't just lend me some? Just a hundred or so, in case anything terrible happens in Bombay and I get stuck.'

'Okay,' Aaron said. He had to think for a minute to work out the details. 'It means I'll have to go to the bank again, as soon as it opens. It'll be a bit tight to do it in the time, but if I go ahead and you meet me in Calingute with my bag, we should still make it to Margoa for the train.'

'You're a saint,' Nick said, his eyelids drooping as he dropped off into a contented doze.

Aaron waited half an hour for Nick in Calingute, before getting into a taxi and coming back to the Gregory Garden, where he found Nick on the veranda with a beer in his hand.

'Where were you?' Aaron was so angry that tiny specks of spit were coming out of the corners of his mouth.

'I was here,' Nick said, in innocent astonishment. 'Where else would I be?'

'I'm going to miss my fucking train.'

'Sorry darling. I had a bhang lassi. I wasn't expecting it to be so strong. I've been unconscious for the last two hours.' He laughed, to show that there had been no harm intended.

Anthony emerged, and assured them that they could still get to Margoa in time if they left immediately.

During the taxi ride Aaron, whose fury had not subsided, but had, if anything, increased in response to Nick's stoned carelessness, kept saying, 'One thing. I only asked you to do one fucking thing, and you couldn't get off that fucking veranda.'

'You knew where I'd be.'

'Exactly.'

'Please,' Nick said, beginning to see through the veils of the drug. 'Can we not be like this, when you're going away and I won't see you again for fuck knows how long? I can't bear it. I had to take that lassi. I needed it. I had to take something. I was shaking. I can't bear the thought of being apart from you. I was going to pieces and I had to steady myself. I thought it was just going to chill me out a little, but it was so strong that I couldn't move. You know what that stuff can be like. Please. It wasn't my fault.'

Aaron was looking out of the window at the palm trees and paddy fields and the drongos on the power lines. He knew that Nick was right about one thing – if they parted under these circumstances he would regret it. He began to reason that Nick must love him an awful lot to have been in such a state about him going. Without turning, he reached his hand across the seat to Nick's and gripped it. 'Do you really love me that much?' he asked.

'Really,' Nick said, as the taxi swerved around a bullock

cart on a blind corner, hooting cheerfully. 'And if we get out of this alive, I'll prove it to you.'

Nick didn't like the look of the train much. It was a rusty old thing with bars on the windows, through which coffee and snacks and money were exchanged and the hands of beggars reached with feigned timidity. There were hard vinyl-covered seats and Aaron was sharing his compartment with an entire family and what looked like half their household goods, wrapped in cardboard and string.

'Couldn't you get a place in first class?' Nick asked, as Aaron stowed his small bag and smiled at the pan-chewing matriarch who hogged the window seat with her feet tucked beneath her, wiping her children's noses with the end of her sari and shouting instructions at her relatives on the platform.

'There isn't a first class on this. Besides, I always go second class sleeper. I prefer it.'

'You can't.'

'It's heaven,' Aaron said, looking about him as if it were.

Nick had often heard him extol the virtues of train travel, and how it was the best way of seeing the world. It had sounded to Nick like the sort of thing you might do once, but only to be able to say you had done it. Now, he was no longer sure that he'd be able to cope with it, even for the sake of anecdote. He was thankful to be able to go home in a nice jumbo jet, with a bar service and toiletries and a film to watch between meals.

'I wish you were coming,' Aaron said. 'You'd love Mysore. Goa isn't the real India.'

Nick shrugged. 'Another time,' he said. 'We'll come back and do it all properly.' He didn't like to say that his idea of doing it properly excluded second class sleepers on an antediluvian train. It wasn't the right moment, somehow, to be raising doubts in Aaron's mind about the polarity of their expectations in life.

The sight of Aaron, as the train moved away, leaning out of an open door, hanging on with one hand and waving with the other, beaming as if he were going on an adventure, was too much for Nick. He cried buckets. He blubbed and sniffed so loudly that a girl came up and touched him on the shoulder, asking him if something was wrong, in a grave, Teutonic accent.

'That's my boyfriend,' he howled. 'He's off round the world and I won't see him for months.'

'Never mind,' she said. 'Head up, even when the collar is dirty.' She followed her *non sequitur* by producing a roll of lavatory paper from her rucksack and encouraging Nick to blow his nose, and then held his hand as the train rounded a bend and Aaron disappeared from view. 'Will you be all right now?'

Nick asked her if she knew of a bar nearby. He needed a drink to steady his nerves.

Nick had never been so relieved to get back to the Gregory Garden. He had found Margoa a nightmare of squalor and traffic. If that was anything like the real India, he thought, then Aaron could keep it. He struggled onto the veranda, which had already been annexed by Cathy, and flaked out in a chair, exhausted after the stresses of the day. Cathy seemed unaccountably cheerful.

'Ferret-face finally gone, has he?' she asked.

'I miss him so much,' Nick said. 'Already.'

LIFE ∫

It was not much of a homecoming. Things started well enough, when Cathy and Nick stumbled through the airport, dazed from vodka miniatures and jet lag. Nick said that he couldn't face the thought of public transport and that they might as well put some of Aaron's money to good use, so they took a taxi into the city, shivering in the back and pulling on cigarettes like junkies in the daylight. He had been away for long enough for his own universe to have become the alien one. The people seemed pallid and hurrying, and the streets themselves had a hard and sterile look he'd never noticed before. It was one of those bright winter days when the sky is pale and the light diffuse and all the colours are variations of shiny grey. During the journey they opened the bags and piled on more and more layers of inadequately thin clothing, until their arms were akimbo and they looked like home-sewn dolls.

'I want to go back,' Nick said. 'This place is dead. We could be sitting on the veranda now, with the heat dripping off us.'

'Saturday night,' Cathy answered. 'Priapus.'

'I couldn't. I couldn't go clubbing tonight. I'm not up to it. And it wouldn't be the same without Aaron.'

'Bloody Aaron again.' She scowled. 'Can't we talk about anything without you bringing him into it?'

'I can't help it. I think about him all the time. I'll be living like a monk until he gets back.'

Cathy sucked her cheeks in and turned her mouth down for one of her more cynical faces, but Nick didn't rise to it.

He decided that he would show her, over the next few weeks, what real love was all about. He was going to pine.

The taxi turned right by the market and into Lennox Street. The Twisted Arms came into view.

'I wonder who'll be in there,' Nick said.

Cathy looked at her watch. 'Most of the crowd by now, I expect.'

Nick thought about striding in, just as they were, brown skin and dripping with Tibetan silver, and the looks on the faces of all the people who'd been stuck at home for the winter. He couldn't resist a grand entrance. 'Stop here,' he said to the driver. 'No. Right outside the pub.' He wanted everyone to be looking out of the windows as he and Cathy stepped from the cab. Cathy was smirking at him. 'We should go in for a quick one,' he said. 'Especially if I'm not going out tonight.'

Nick often said that the Twisted Arms was like a second home to him. Although he had lived in a lot of houses and flats over the previous ten years, it had been his local for most of that time. He liked to have somewhere that he could just walk into on any day of the week, where there would always be someone he could talk to. There was never a shortage of conversational subject matter: who'd got off with what, and who'd split up, and who was back together again even though they should have known better. There was always someone to stand a pint if you were broke and someone to buy a drink for if you were flush.

The pub was packed. Nick and Cathy made a pile of their bags in the middle of the floor and people squeezed through the crowd to yell hello to them over the din. Nick became instantly euphoric. He had walked in off the dead of winter street and was immediately catapulted into the middle of a steaming party. Everyone wanted to know what India had been like and he told them how fabulous it was, and how you could get valium and speed over the counter at the chemist's and be jerked off for a quid by the beach masseur, and how the drugs were so cheap that you could be off your face the entire time and still live like a king. Before he knew it, the day was gone and it was closing time. A lot of people were going to Priapus, so he asked Rhona, the landlady, if she'd hang on to the bags until the morning. Rhona said that was fine by her, she'd do anything for her best customer, and he and Cathy changed in the toilets and were ready to go.

On the way up the street his friend Danielle linked her arm through his and said, 'I'm glad you're back. The place wasn't the same without you.' Then she hesitated a little and Nick was about to say something about Aaron, and how he couldn't wait for everyone to meet his new boyfriend, but she asked, nervously, 'You know all that valium you were talking about?'

'Yes?' He couldn't help sounding cautious.

'I don't know if you heard what was going on between Ed and me while you were away.'

Someone had been saying something about them earlier, but he hadn't been listening properly. Now that he looked at her, she did seem a bit thin and panda-eyed. 'No,' he said. 'Have I told you about Aaron yet?'

She cut him short, managing to sound apologetic about it at the same time. 'I had an abortion at Christmas. It was all a bit much. I'm having real problems sleeping.'

'Can't the doctor give you something?'

'She did. She prescribed mazzies for me, but Ed's swallowed the lot. You know what he's like with drugs around.'

'Uh,' Nick said. He had a feeling he knew what was coming next.

'You couldn't let me have a few valium? Just enough to get me through the weekend. I'm desperate.'

'Sweetie,' he said. 'I wish I could help, but I didn't bring any back. I didn't want to risk it at Customs. You know what I'm like. I get very nervous about that sort of thing.' He kissed Danielle on the head as they walked along. 'You'll be fine,' he said. 'You've got your friends. Anytime you want to talk about it, just tell me. Listening is what I do best.' Then he told her about Aaron, and how they'd met and how much he was looking forward to seeing him again, and how good-looking and clever and famous he was. As soon as he could, without making it seem too obvious, he dropped behind Danielle and took Cathy aside to warn her not to let on that they'd brought drugs back, because Danielle was on the scrounge.

Cathy said, 'D'you think I was born yesterday?'

Ahead of them, Danielle had caught up with Ed and taken his arm. Ed was the cute plumber's mate type, always good for a laugh. 'Typical of him,' Nick said, 'to nick all the mazzies when Danielle is obviously on the verge of a nervous breakdown for want of sleep. Some men are so selfish you wonder how they get anyone to stay with them. I mean, what a position to put me in. I need those valium. If the Twisted Arms crowd find out that we have a stockpile they'll all be round. Those people are like leeches, always after a free drink as soon as they think you've got money in your pocket.'

'Oh give it a rest,' Cathy said. 'You sound like a one man phone-in.'

The queue outside Priapus went right round the block and into Dury Street. Most of the people from the pub had to go and stand at the end of it. Nick never queued, and neither did Cathy. One or the other of them could always find a way to blag themselves in. If all else failed, Nick had a fake identity card from The Sound Factory and that would get them in almost anywhere. They knew him better than that at Priapus.

Elvira, the door whore, was looking a bit hassled.

'Hello sweetie,' Nick said, but Elvira just scowled at him and went on fluttering at his clipboard. It was one of those rare situations for Nick when the truth seemed the best tactic. 'We just got back from India this afternoon, so we're not on the guestlist. Is there anything spare?'

'Oh it's you,' Elvira said, without looking up from his lists. 'I didn't know you, you got so brown. How did you manage to put on weight in India?'

Cathy said, 'Don't be a cunt and just let us in.' She and Elvira went back a long way.

The pleasure of that moment had never worn off for Nick, when he waltzed in with all the queue glaring at him and wondering how he had done it, and again, a few minutes later, when he barged straight to the counter at the coat check. There was generally someone he'd shagged working in there. He and Cathy had a system in clubs. She would go for the drinks while he made a beeline for the dealer. Then, as soon as the E was down their necks, they would go upstairs, if it was Priapus, and sit out on the gantry over the dancefloor until the drug started to come up, squinting down to see who was there and what they were up to.

He often said that Priapus was also like a second home to him. He had worked there once, as a busboy, which was how he knew so many of the staff. It was a huge place, having once been a church. The stage was where the altar must have been and the upstairs bars were in the former galleries. Cages were suspended over the dancefloor, in which muscular strippers danced, waving their cocks at the crowd below. The floor was a heaving mass of sweaty torsos, and divas lined up on the edge of the stage, eyes bulging with ecstasy and arms flailing in the air. Nick rarely missed a Saturday. Even at his lowest ebb he could find something to cheer him up in that place. As the E began to kick in, all he could think was that he wished Aaron were with him.

There is something about being in love that makes people more attractive. It may be the stupid smile. Whatever it was, Nick was pleased to be able to say that he could have gone home with any one of half a dozen good-looking men that night. He may have been flirting a little, out of habit. That was part of the fun of being out. When it came to the crunch, however, he would always peel the man off him and say, 'Look, if I was single I'd love to have sex with you, but I've got a boyfriend and I don't think he'd be too keen on this.'

Sometime between three and four Nick came across his flatmate, Paul, on the dancefloor. The second white diamond was coming along nicely, with the help of a judicious wrap of whizz which he'd nicked from someone who was too off his face to notice, and Nick hardly knew where he was, tripping on the lazers and gazing upwards at his favourite stripper. There was a tap on his shoulder and Paul was standing there, saying, 'I heard you were back,' or something like it. He seemed a bit peeved.

For a seventeen year old, Paul was way ahead of his years, in some respects. He made a living and he had no trouble spending his money. In other ways, according to Nick, he was just a big, sulky child. When Nick had first moved into Paul's flat he had euphemised the arrangement by saying that he was taking Paul under his wing. Subsequently, Nick was constantly complaining to his friends that Paul had become a bit too dependent, treating Nick like the father he'd never had, expecting Nick to fuck him on demand and so forth. Fucking Paul was the nearest that Nick came to paying rent, but there was no question of theirs being anything other than an open relationship, given what Paul did for a living. Though the relationship served its purposes in the short term, Nick knew that it had to be finite. Paul, on the other hand, had told Nick that he was in love with him, and had become possessive. Going to India, as far as Nick was concerned, had been a way of giving them both a breathing space. Now, from the look on Paul's face, Nick could tell that nothing had changed and Paul was pissed off because Nick hadn't gone straight to the flat from the airport. Fortunately, Nick had taken too many drugs to do anything but smile, which gave the impression that he was pleased to see Paul.

'Some bloke was round this evening,' Paul said. 'Looking for you.' At least, that's what Nick thought he said. It was hard to tell on the dancefloor, above the noise of the music, even when someone was shouting in his ear.

'What sort of bloke?'

'I dunno. Posh.'

Nick should have asked what the bloke's name was, but he got a big rush just at that moment and, Paul being the nearest thing to hand, Nick put his arms around him as though he was the love of his life. Then the giant balloons came floating down from the ceiling and everyone had their arms in the air and the music went completely mad. As he got the poppers out, Nick shouted at Paul, 'I love this place. There's nothing like this anywhere else.'

At half past six, when the music stopped and the lights came up, Cathy found Nick. 'On your own?' she asked, with a coyness he wasn't going to dignify with a reply. 'Paul is looking for you.'

'Oh fuck,' he said. He wasn't up to dealing with that. Paul had asked him if he was going back to the flat afterwards, and Nick had said of course he was. Knowing the score the way she did, Cathy could be relied on in this situation. 'You keep an eye out for him,' Nick said. 'I'll get the coats. If you see him, tell him I've gone back to the flat already.'

They saw Paul in the queue for coats but, luckily, he was a long way back and talking to someone and didn't see them. Nick and Cathy had a good twenty minute start on him.

Outside, it was a drizzly, blanket-dark morning, the hint of what passes for dawn in winter only adding to the gloom. The cab drivers crowded round, touting for business. Nick asked Cathy if she had any money left.

'No. Have you?'

'Of course I bloody haven't. When have I ever come out of that place with money?' Suddenly, Nick hated being home. He missed the sunshine after a night out in Goa, and the feeling that money was limitless and you could buy anything you wanted. They walked back to Cathy's in silence, drips of cold water hanging from the ends of their noses.

Sunday got lost, somehow, in the way that Sundays do. They went to the Twisted Arms at opening time to collect their bags, and Rhona gave them a welcome home pint, and Nick borrowed a tenner from Danielle and Ed, and then there was a lock-in for the holy hour. Nick wasn't aware of much beyond a general feeling of comfortable moroseness. He said he was missing Aaron, repeatedly. If Aaron had been there he wouldn't have had to go back to Paul's flat. There was a new life in a nice house, tantalisingly nearby, and long rainy months to get through before he could have it.

At closing time Nick thought it might be safe to go home. Paul usually worked on Sunday nights so, even if he'd brought a client back, he wouldn't be able to talk, and certainly couldn't demand sex.

The street Nick lived on was one of those which is perpetually on the brink of gentrification, but never quite makes it. Young couples moved in and started buying stripped pine furniture and mud-resist duvet covers, and then a stray bullet from some crack dealer shoot-out would penetrate their newly restored period windows and suddenly life on the front line wasn't so amusing. Almost every house on the street had terracotta windowboxes which were now cracked and sprawling with dead weeds. It was an area where the rubbish didn't stay in the bins and the wind was more likely to take it away than the council.

Nick tackled the three locks on the reinforced door, standing ankle-deep in cans and paper, and his nerve almost failed him. If he'd had somewhere else to go, he would have gone. The lightbulb had not been replaced in the hall and there was a familiar, dismaying smell of catshit and old vomit. A lot of that vomit would have been his own, between one thing and another. He had got into the habit of always throwing up in the same place when he got home of an evening, never seeming to make it the last twenty feet to the bathroom. He had to hold his breath on the way up the stairs, not to be sick again. He'd told Paul to buy a new carpet, but Paul said it was the landlord's job. This one was like random mouse-skins held together with strands of brown twine. 'Fucking deathtrap,' he muttered, as he stumbled up.

There were voices coming from the sitting room as he opened the flat door. Remembering what Paul had said about a bloke who wanted to see him, Nick thought of slipping away again until the identity of the caller had been established. Nine times out of ten, in Nick's experience, someone who was actively searching him out was the last person he would want to be found by. He picked his bags up again and began to move backwards, but Paul had heard his key in the lock and his face was glaring down at Nick from the sitting room doorway before the retreat had been completed.

'It's him,' Paul said. 'He's here.' It was hard to know whether the information was being directed at Nick or at the visitor, since it applied to both of them. The next remark, however, was unmistakably directed at Nick, as Paul stamped off towards his room, shouting, 'I'm going to want an explanation for this, and it better be fucking good.'

Nick was left to face whatever horror was waiting for him. He froze, maybe in the primitive hope that the danger he was up against might ignore him if he stood still enough. His mind raced through all the people who were out to get him, trying to fix on one who could be described as posh. There were at least three possibilities, and none of them comforting. Hung with luggage, pissed and terrorstruck, Nick remained rooted to the spot for a full three seconds. Aaron appeared, dressed in fine, soft, expensive grey, the depth of his tan at odds with the winter clothing. His face bore an expression that might have been described as worried. Nick was struck by how beautiful he was. He had remembered Aaron as handsome and sexy, but had never before thought of the word beautiful in conjunction with him. Nick was thinking, in an inebriated way, 'This is my man. This is the love of my life.' He worried that Aaron must be looking at him and thinking what a terrible mistake the whole thing had been. Feeling a compulsion to say something, and in the way that the worst thing always comes out at the most crucial moment, Nick asked, 'What are you doing here?'

Without a word, Aaron came down the stairs, and Nick dropped his bags to the floor, and Aaron held him.

The family who shared Aaron's compartment on the train from Margoa were going to Bangalore. They had a fantastic, very fat baby in a gold frock. The baby wore a lot of make-up, and was so used to having kohl put on its eyes that it would continue sleeping while its mother pulled the eyelids down and smudged the black stuff in. Aaron had to think of it as an it, because he couldn't tell what sex it might be and, imagining this might be due to some basic cultural ignorance on his part, was afraid to ask in case he caused offence. The family, on the other hand, pressed him with all the usual questions which are asked of tourists on trains, the first of which was whether he was married.

Without thinking about it too much, Aaron answered that he was, since his involvement with Nick made him feel as though he was. They had, in his estimate, made as many and as profound commitments to each other in private as those made by married people in public.

'Where is your good wife?' It was the father of the family who asked the questions, though they were all listening carefully to the answers and commenting on them to each other in Kannada. The women were hennaing each other's hands.

'In Goa,' Aaron answered, a little shiftily, seeing that he might have been wiser to give a less metaphoric answer.

'Why does your good wife not travel with you?' The man asked, astonished that anyone would travel alone by choice. The women were looking at Aaron with something that might, at any moment, become disapproval, depending on his answer.

Aaron decided to lie. 'She is sick.'

This, at first, produced a wave of sympathy in the compartment and much discussion, at the end of which the matriarch pressed her husband to ask a further question. 'Why do you not stay in Goa to look after your sick good wife?'

The good wife business was getting a bit much for Aaron, and he was tempted to give them a quick burst of the facts, at the risk of outraging their moral sensibilities. However, he knew that he had another twenty-three hours of close confinement with these people, and that the journey would not be better for any of them if he made a complete pariah of himself through honesty. He was inspired to say, 'I am going to Mysore for medicine.'

There was a chorus of *achas* and a general agreement that there were very good doctors in Mysore.

'And your good friend who was weeping terribly at the railway station?'

'My wife's brother,' Aaron said, hurriedly. Now that the fiction had some substance to it, it was easier to flesh out the details. 'He will look after her until I get back.'

'*Acha.*' The melodrama was beginning to run along lines which the family could sympathise with. 'How many children do you have?'

'None,' Aaron said, relieved by this factual tangent.

There was some clucking among the women, and a pitying look or two. The man actually said that he was sorry to hear it.

'We've only been married a month,' Aaron said. 'We are on honeymoon.' Too late, he realised that it might seem odd to have brought his brother-in-law on honeymoon, but he needn't have worried. It did not occur to anyone else that there was anything unreasonable in bringing as many family members as you could cram in on any expedition.

Dudhsagar Falls came into view and the train slowed to a halt so that the passengers could admire the view. Aaron took the opportunity to leave the compartment and end his interrogation. He sat on the floor in one of the open doorways, with his legs dangling from the side of the train, and stayed there until after dark, watching the landscape and thinking about Nick.

Their last morning had been a disaster. He tried to think of reasons why it should have been so. He told himself that little things got out of proportion when strong feelings were involved. He told himself that it had been no accident they had both been miserable at the prospect of so much time apart. He convinced himself that it had been his own fault for being so angry, for overreacting. The most obvious possibility – that in falling in love with Nick he had made a bad choice – was not something he was prepared to countenance, for the moment.

Mysore seemed a different city to the one he had left a month before. The same things were in the same places. The market was still full of flowers and smells and the generators still hummed outside the silk shops during power cuts, but none of it was quite so interesting or diverting. He was miserable. He ascribed this misery to missing his lover, but there was something more to it than that. He was beginning to entertain his doubts seriously. Obsessively, he thought about the previous morning, and the more he thought about it, the more it appeared to him that there had been something fundamentally wrong in Nick's behaviour. Once he had thought that, it was a short step to considering the business about the threesome with Jason, and the business of never getting off the veranda, and the whole multi-conglomerate corporation of Nick's attitude to sex.

Everything was falling apart. He bought a ticket for the Maharaja's palace and shuffled round, barefoot, pretending to gawp at the ornaments like any tourist, but his mind was a battlefield of argument, which always came back to the same question, louder and louder until he began to mutter it under his breath. Inevitably he eventually asked it a little too loud, and with a sort of angry insistence, to the bewilderment of a group of schoolchildren who were standing nearby.

'Who are you?' he asked.

'It is the Lord Ganesh,' one of the children answered, taking him literally, since he was standing in front of a marble statue of the elephant-headed god.

Embarrassed, Aaron thanked the child and hurried for the exit, the children shrieking with laughter behind him.

He decided that he was going mad. His journey was wrecked. There was no question of seeing the world when all he could see was Nick standing in front of him. He climbed Chaimundi Hill, with the vision of Nick before him, and with every one of the thousand steps he asked, 'Who are you?' When he stood at the top, with his calf muscles aching, he knew what he had to do. There was going to be no peace of mind until he had seen Nick.

Once he had made the decision, an enveloping calm settled on him, which convinced him that he was doing the right thing. His first plan was to try and catch Nick in Goa, and he went to the Indian Airline offices, but the flights to Goa were full. The second idea was to go to Bombay, where Nick was to change planes, but the flights there were full too. He tried to phone the Gregory Garden, but something somewhere wasn't working and he couldn't get through. Each obstacle made him more determined to get to Nick somehow, and it was in this blind determination that he arranged a flight home, which would arrive on the Saturday evening, not many hours after Nick's.

It wasn't until he was on the plane that he realised the

full implications of what he had done. He had sacrificed half the journey of a lifetime. It was no good saying that he could return to Mysore and pick up where he had left off. The whole point of the journey had been to lose himself. Going home now was like having a lunch break during Ramadan. He felt as though he had given up, and his only hope was that whatever was going on between him and Nick was worth it.

Cynicism kept creeping in. He would think of all the things he had said to Nick and realise, with an unbearable clarity, that he had said those things to other people; that they had been said as much in hope as in conviction. He wanted to believe that there was something different about this love; something that would make it work; make it fit into his expectation of a perfect universe. He needed to believe that he had been right. He thought, for some reason, that if he saw Nick again his questions would be answered and his faith restored.

He went straight to Nick's flat from the airport. In answer to the bell a youth stuck his head out of an upstairs window and asked him what he wanted.

'Nick Lovely,' he said.

'He's not back,' the youth replied, flatly, and withdrew.

Aaron went home and spent a restless night. He didn't want to call anyone because he couldn't have explained why he had returned. The house had a dead feel to it, the deep quiet that houses acquire when no one has used them for a while. He called round to Nick's twice more on the Sunday, and Paul let him in on his third visit. They had just begun, warily, to establish each other's credentials when Nick came home.

The bedraggled man at the foot of the stairs was so unlike the vision he had been questioning in Mysore, that Aaron, momentarily, failed to recognise his lover. He covered his confusion with the embrace. Once he was holding Nick,

all the doubts and frustrations dissolved, appearing to have
been no more than a mechanism to get him home, and
an excuse to have Nick in his arms again, where he
belonged.

Holding tight, there were a few moments when, as far as both of them were concerned, if they never spoke or moved again the rest of their lives would be perfect.

Nick was the first to resurface from this delusion. 'Let's get out of here,' he said. It had occurred to him that Paul might have been saying all kinds of things about him. He needed to be alone with Aaron and ask a few careful questions before he could know which line to take in defence of himself. Even if nothing had been said, he couldn't trust Paul not to come charging out of his room and make a scene. Besides all that, the flat looked like a student's kip. There was a pile of empty pizza boxes on the landing. Through the open bathroom door he could see discarded towels and underpants, and he had a fair idea what sort of state the kitchen would be in. Paul was not inclined to wash up or put things away unless Nick made him do it. Housework, in that flat, involved Nick losing his temper when the mess became disgusting, and Paul slamming things into piles or plastic bags, while grumbling at having to do all the work, and getting in the way of the television as much as possible so that Nick would notice the effort he was making. It was not the impression that Nick wanted to give Aaron of the way he lived.

'I'll call a cab,' Nick said.

'No need. I've got the car outside.'

'You parked in this street? At night?'

'Why not?'

'We'll probably have to call the police and a cab. Take these.' Nick handed Aaron two of his bags to carry down, while he put the rest in his room, which was in exactly the condition he'd left it in on the morning he left for India. 'You lazy bastard,' he muttered. 'You couldn't even make my bed to welcome me home.'

Aaron was waiting in the street by an old yellow Capri.

'Where's your car?' Nick asked.

'This is it.'

Nick hesitated and looked up and down the street for something smarter, suspecting a joke, but Aaron was already getting behind the wheel of the Capri. 'No wonder it wasn't stolen,' he said, as he slithered into the passenger seat and sat with his elbows pressed to his sides and his knees together, as though the car might contaminate him in some way. 'Why does nothing ever go right in my life?'

'What's the matter?' Aaron asked, reaching for his hand as he turned the motor on.

'Nothing. Why?'

'You don't seem very pleased to see me.'

Nick was close to tears. It was nothing to do with being pleased or not pleased to see Aaron, it was just that he wouldn't have planned it this way. 'It's the shock, that's all,' he said. 'I thought you were supposed to be squatting on a train somewhere.'

'I know. I'm sorry.'

'I'm not very good at surprises.'

'There was no way of letting you know. I had to see you. I got as far as Mysore and I thought I was going mad, I missed you so much. I thought you might be feeling the same.' Speaking his reasons out loud made them sound feeble to Aaron, but he couldn't admit that it was doubt which had driven him halfway round the world. That would have been too easily misinterpreted. 'I shouldn't have done it, should I?' he asked. 'I should have stuck to the plan.'

'No,' Nick said, mumbling slightly. 'I'm glad you did. I've never been so pleased to see anyone in my life. I'm just not used to anyone being this nice. This is the best thing that anyone has ever done for me.'

'That's all right then.'

'It scares me.' Nick sounded as though he were half asleep. 'How am I going to cope with being loved this intensely for the rest of my life?'

Aaron said that he'd just have to get used to it, but there was no answer. Nick was asleep.

Though the distance was short, the street where Aaron lived could not have been more different, in terms of respectability, from the one they had left behind. There were front gardens and hedges and Neighbourhood Watch stickers, and windowboxes where pansies and crocuses grew. Aaron shook his passenger awake, as gently as if he was breakable, led him inside and put him to bed. Nick had a dim, somnambulant impression of rooms full of books and yellow lamplight and thick, long curtains. He pissed in a bathroom which looked as though it had never been used for anything but the training of charladies, where there were yet more books and a great deep sofa, incongruous on the white tiles. Aaron's bed was sleep-made-material, and Nick was unconscious before his feet had stretched to the end, still aware of Aaron's skin along the length of his back and backside. It felt as though they were flying somewhere, and Aaron was holding him up, safe. This feeling was still extraordinary to Nick, who had rarely known what it was to be unafraid. Had he not been so tired, it might have terrified him.

It was a long sleep, and mid-afternoon when he woke, in a quiet, darkened room, with a pain in his bladder from the drink and an ache in his teeth from the drugs, and jackhammer vibrations in his head from both. Aaron was a patient shadow, sitting on the bed, watching for Nick's eyes to open.

Aaron whispered, 'Hello,' kissed him and went downstairs.

The basin in the bathroom had a bottle of aspirin beside it, and a new toothbrush still in the packet. There was a pile of towels you could have used as a trampoline and hot water was gushing into a bath the size of a small tugboat. By the time Nick had finished he felt as though he was transparent with cleanliness and that the new life had begun.

Aaron called from downstairs, telling him to get back into bed. The curtains had been opened and the bedroom was flooded with light. Nick was desperate to look through the wardrobes, the door of one of which was half-open, disclosing a tantalising row of suit sleeves, but he could hear Aaron coming up the stairs, and had to remind himself that there would be plenty of time for snooping later.

Aaron's idea of a breakfast tray would have put any hotel to shame. Nick stared at it for a long time, thinking how carefully it must have been planned.

'Is something the matter?' Aaron asked. 'Is there something else you'd rather have?'

Nick said that he didn't know what to say; that he wasn't used to this kind of treatment.

'Well you'd better get used to it. This is the way things are done around here.'

Nick said that it was perfect.

'There's nothing wrong with perfection.'

Stuffing a forkful of egg into his mouth, Nick nodded in the direction of the row of sleeves and asked if all the suits were handmade.

'How else would they be made?' Aaron was trying to be modest, but it sounded like semantic nit-picking.

'You know what I mean.'

'Sorry.' Aaron went to close the wardrobe door. 'I'm a bit of a clothes horse.'

At the sight of him from behind, Nick felt a rush of love, and said, 'Will you do me a favour?'

'Anything.' It was said so unhesitatingly that Nick considered taking advantage. It made the hairs stand on the back of his neck to think that he had found a man who would give him anything. He considered asking for a thousand pounds, but even he was capable of realising that it was a bit early to push his luck, so he stuck to the original request he'd had in mind.

'Come back to bed. I want you naked.'

He watched Aaron undress, turned on by the way he was a bit shy about it, as though they had never seen each other naked before, and by the way that Aaron's cock reared as soon as it was looked at. Nick made him stand at the end of the bed and play with himself. Though a little embarrassed, Aaron did it, and his embarrassment only served to make Nick wilder in his masturbation. Nick's eyes careered up and down the details of Aaron's body.

Love makes for real beauty, more than any airbrush can. In a cold light, Aaron's body was ordinary. He was tall and fit and lean, but no taller, fitter or leaner than many other men. His dick, admittedly, was faultless, a rare enough phenomenon. His arse could have won contests and his legs were the sort that would make you bump into lamp posts if you saw them in the street, but still, it was only love that made him seem perfect.

It was not in Nick's nature to admit as much. 'If you worked out for a while you could be a stripper,' he said, as he wiped the spunk off his stomach with Aaron's dressing gown, thinking that to be about as complimentary a remark as anyone was due.

'Sorry,' Aaron said, his erection wilting in his hand.

'Don't worry about it. You're good enough for me.'

'You're staring,' Aaron said, getting into bed to cover his nudity.

'I could stare at you all afternoon. Oh come on, don't get all offended. I was trying to be nice. You obviously don't understand my sense of humour.'

Aaron had to admit that he didn't.

'You'll soon get used to my little ways. Do you want me to suck you off now?'

Aaron grinned bashfully and burrowed down beside him. Though he was erect again, and bursting with it this time, he was not used to sex being dealt with so pragmatically. In India, with the heat and the drugs, lust had seemed more like an itch that could be scratched mechanically, but now that he was in domestic surroundings with a clear mind, he wanted something that was more like love.

Nick had another idea. 'Do you have any porn?' he asked. 'I'd really like to see you jerking off over a porn film, pretending that I'm not in the room. That would really turn me on.'

Aaron had to confess that he didn't own any porn.

'What? Nothing?' Nick made it sound as though it was one of the basic necessities of life. He half disbelieved Aaron and made a mental note to search for the porn later, assuming it must be so disgusting that Aaron was ashamed of it – and therefore something really worth looking at, as an insight into Aaron's libido, if nothing else. 'How can someone as oversexed as you not have porn in the house.'

'I don't like it,' Aaron said, not liking either that he was being made to sound like a prude. 'It turns me on at first, but then I start to think about the people, and whether they're really enjoying what they do.'

'They know what they're doing all right,' Nick said. 'Take it from me. We'll soon cure you of that. I'll bring some over from my place. You just don't know anything about the finer things in life. Yet.'

Aaron thought it best to change the subject by asking Nick what he'd been doing at the weekend. There was no hint of accusation, so Nick started to gabble on about how much he'd missed Aaron and had tried to enjoy himself, but couldn't stop thinking about him, how he'd bored all his friends stupid with talking about him, and about all the men who'd tried to seduce him, but were rebuffed because he was in love and couldn't even think of sleeping with anyone else. When Nick had established that he'd had a rotten time and that life wasn't worth living without Aaron by his side, he felt the moment was right to ask, cautiously, what, if anything, Paul had been saying.

'Nothing. Chit chat. I told him a bit about India. He told me about the course he was doing at college. I liked him.'

'Oh good,' Nick said.

'I couldn't work out what was going on at first. You never told me you had a flatmate.'

'Didn't I? I suppose I don't really think of him as a flatmate. I sort of took him under my wing. His parents kicked him out.' It was just as well, Nick thought, to earn a few Brownie points while the going was good.

'That was nice of you.' Aaron was one of those people who felt guilty about the homeless. He was full of admiration for someone who was prepared to help on such a practical and selfless level.

'I know,' Nick said. 'I can be too kind for my own good. People take advantage. I don't feel at home in my own flat these days.'

'Is he a problem?'

Nick shrugged. 'You know what young people can be like.'

'I think,' Aaron said, with the weight of someone who

imagines that he is making a useful remark, 'Paul has a bit of a crush on you.'

'Tell me about it,' Nick said, wearily.

'What age is he?'

'Nearly eighteen.' Nick felt he had to tell the truth about that, since Aaron was bound to find out sooner or later. Though it was only a sliver of veracity, it made Nick realise that there were one or two other things he should reveal, to get his version established before Aaron was exposed to the gossipmongers. 'As far as I know,' he said, 'Paul's on the game.'

'No?' Aaron made it sound like the worst kind of tragedy.

Nick was tempted to laugh at the strength of Aaron's reaction, but composed himself in time. 'I know,' he said, gravely.

'Can't you help him?'

'I do what I can.' That, Nick felt, was true, in the strictest sense. He had introduced Paul to some of his best contacts. Before Nick moved in, the boy had been running his business in a completely haphazard fashion and not charging nearly enough.

'I suppose,' Aaron said, 'he's lucky to know you, what with you having been through the same thing and all.'

'Exactly.'

'Do you think you can get him to give it up?'

'No. I know what it's like. You can't be told any-thing when you're that age. He's making easy money and getting himself through college, and it all seems like a bit of a lark to him. I just try to be there for him, and make sure that he doesn't get into anything stupid.'

Aaron had to think about that for a bit, before adding, 'And at least he has someone to talk to.'

'Exactly,' Nick said. He was tired of talking about Paul.

He leaned across to the window and looked down into the street. 'That car,' he said, 'will have to go.'

Aaron looked hurt. 'What's wrong with my car?'

'What's right with it? It's old. It's tacky. Don't think that I'm going to be seen stepping out of that, matey. I don't like being laughed at.'

'I love my car.' Aaron had drawn away, and the expression on his face showed confusion as much as disappointment, like a creature being punished for a transgression it has forgotten.

Nick recognised a stalemate looming ahead of them. The car issue would have to be deferred for the moment. 'Come here,' he said, 'and don't be such a baby. I was only joking. Can't you take a joke? There, you see, I told you you didn't understand my sense of humour.'

Aaron allowed an embrace. Nick was laughing at him, and his awkwardness, and the injured way in which he had defended his precious car. 'So,' Aaron said, making an effort not to sound any more foolish than he had already been made out to be, 'what do you really think? About the car.'

'It's beautiful. Very unusual. I suppose it could be seen as a sort of anti-fashion chic.'

'No,' Aaron said. 'I just like it. The first time I saw it I knew it was the car for me. I had a boring BMW then. What sort of car do you have?'

'I'm sort of between cars at the moment.' Nick decided to be dismissive. 'You know what it's like in the city. They're more trouble than they're worth.'

'How do you get away at weekends?'

'Get away where? To the country?' Nick was trying to keep the note of hysteria out of his voice at the thought of a Saturday night up to his knees in mud, when he could be at Priapus, up to his neck in muscle. 'Oh, you know. I manage. Somehow. There's always someone with a car. There's always the train.'

'I'd better put you on the insurance. Then we can share the driving.'

Nick didn't think it appropriate, just then, to tell Aaron that he didn't have a licence. Besides which, that detail had never stopped him driving in the past.

They spent the rest of the day talking. Aaron showed no sign of resentment at having missed half the world to be there. It was, he said, a treat to be in his own house when no one knew he was home; with no work to do and without the phone ringing every five minutes. He was more concerned that he was keeping Nick away from his projects. Nick had given the impression, while they were in Goa, that he would be caught up in a tornado of meetings and negotiations the moment he got back, which made Aaron think that it was very generous of him to be spending the day in bed.

Nick said, vaguely, that while he had been out on Saturday he had met some of the people he was working with. The finance had fallen through and everything was on the back burner for the moment. There was no rush. He said that this was just as well, since it gave them more time to spend together, and plan the future.

Then, adroitly, he asked Aaron a question which had been bothering him since he had woken. 'Why isn't there a television in this bedroom?'

Aaron said that there wasn't a television in the house at all; that he used to have one, but never had time to watch it, so he had given it away.

That was when Nick knew that he couldn't put off going back to the flat. Given a choice between facing up to Paul and facing a life without television, there was no contest.

'We'll stay at my place tonight,' he said.

Being so cossetted at Aaron's made Nick forget the harsher realities of his life. He realised, as soon as he was through the door of his flat, what a bad suggestion it had been that they go there. Paul was lying in wait for him, and not a bit pleased to see that he wasn't alone. He wouldn't say anything while Aaron was there, but made his feelings clear by banging doors and clattering in the kitchen and scowling. After five minutes, Nick said that he couldn't stand it any more and took Aaron down to the Twisted Arms.

Monday nights were always slack, but Ed was there, watching the football. He kept his eyes on the screen while Nick told him about the problems they were having. Anyone else might think that he wasn't interested, but Nick knew him better. Occasionally, Ed would say something germaine out of the corner of his mouth.

'He's only a kid,' he said. 'What do you expect?'

'There's no excuse for that sort of behaviour. He could, at least, be polite to Aaron, no matter how he feels about me. It was horrible, wasn't it?' Nick looked at Aaron for confirmation, and Aaron shrugged his shoulders. 'It was really upsetting. When I think of all I've done for him, and now that I have a chance of real happiness all he cares about is himself. I feel I can't go back to my own flat.'

Ed slid his eyes away from the screen for a moment. 'Kick

him out then,' he said, deadpan, knowing that Nick was in no position to do it. Nick had been sleeping on Ed and Danielle's sofa before he had moved in with Paul.

Aaron, feeling that this was being hard on the homeless, said, 'You can't do that. Where would he go? You can always stay at my place until he calms down a little.'

Only someone who knew Ed as well as Nick did, would have realised he was laughing at something. He made no sound, and the only features to change shape were his eyes, which creased slightly. He held his empty glass out to Nick and said, 'There you are. Problem solved. Have you got the tenner you owe me?'

'Not on me, at the moment,' Nick said, passing the glass, along with his own, on to Aaron, as an indication that he should go to the bar.

After closing time they paid another brief visit to the flat, to collect Nick's television and a few other essentials, before returning to the house with the book-padded walls. Paul managed to trap Nick on his own for a moment, while Aaron was loading stuff into the car.

'What the fuck's going on? Are you moving out?'

'No,' Nick said. 'Of course not.' He still wanted to keep his options covered. 'I'm just going over to his place for a few nights. Look, this might be the big one. We both knew that this was likely to happen. We said from the start that we should only stay together until something better came along, you know we did. We talked about it before I went to India.'

'So when are you going to pay me back for that?'

'Is that all you care about? Money? You go on about how much you love me, but when my life's happiness is at stake all you can talk about is a couple of thousand measly pounds. Money you wouldn't have earned if it wasn't for me in the first place. Anyway, you gave me that money.'

'I lent it to you. And now I want it back.'

Nick could hear Aaron on the stairs. There wasn't time to argue. 'You'll get your fucking blood money,' he hissed, and went down to head Aaron off.

Aaron noticed the rage Nick was in as they drove away.

'Is it Paul?' he asked.

'Why can't people just leave us alone? They see how happy we are with each other and they're jealous, that's what it is.'

'Don't get too worked up about it. He's dependent on you and he's worried he's going to lose you. When he sees that I'm not a threat, that you're still a good friend to him, he'll be fine. You've just got to let him know that I'm on his side.'

Nick wanted to tell Aaron that he was talking shit, but he couldn't, since Aaron was drawing conclusions from the facts which Nick had given him. It was easier to carry on from where they were. 'It isn't just Paul. It was the way Cathy was, and everyone else in Goa. I could see the way that Ed was looking at you tonight.'

'He seemed fine to me.'

'You don't know him. He obviously thought you were a posh git, for a start. People like him can't stand to see anyone else having a nice time.'

'Well,' Aaron said, 'none of my friends are so small minded.'

Aaron intended to sound reassuring rather than conceited, but Nick took him as being the latter, sneering at him for having inferior friends while all Aaron's friends, like everything else in his life, were perfect. Nick could have hit him for his arrogance, but Aaron was driving, and Nick was just about sober enough to know that he'd be putting both their lives in danger.

Which reminded him, 'Should you be driving when you've been drinking? What if we're stopped?'

Aaron was taken aback by Nick's snappish tone. 'I've only had one pint,' he protested.

'One pint, bollocks. We were in there for over an hour. You went up to the bar three times.'

'Yes, and I only had one pint. Didn't you notice? I don't drink as fast as you.'

Aaron was sounding riled, so Nick backed off. 'If you say so,' he said, in a voice sarcastic with disbelief. 'Mr bloody perfect,' he mumbled.

'What was that?'

'Nothing.'

Nick had calmed down by the time they arrived at the house, and came near to saying he was sorry. 'It wasn't my fault. Paul had a go at me and shook me up a bit. And then I was worried because I knew I wasn't fit to drive and I assumed you were in the same condition, and I love you so much that the thought of anything happening to you makes me angry. Can we just pretend that tonight didn't happen? Please? Let's just stay out of everyone's way for the next few weeks. Everything's perfect when it's just you and me. It's other people that are the problem.'

To Nick, this was a rational explanation. He listened to his own words as they came out and they made sense of his behaviour. He had a talent for believing whatever he said, at the moment he was saying it – and afterwards, if necessary. As far as he was concerned, the only criterion for a statement to be true was that it should be believable. Fortunately for him, he was a persuasive arguer. Aaron could see nothing unacceptable in his excuse, and so smiled, and said that they were both tired and should go to bed.

Nick suggested a nightcap first. He watched as Aaron opened the large square cupboard between the two windows of the sitting room. The cupboard was oak and the inside was filled with bottles and half bottles; the remnants of years of duty free and presents brought by guests. There was just about every alcoholic drink imaginable, and enough, Nick suspected, to fuel a two day party. All of his life he had dreamed of having a house with a drinks cupboard like that. It was so civilised; such an indication of restraint and good living. In the circles Nick frequented you didn't go to bed until you had finished whatever drink had come through the door. Nothing he could have seen in that house, not even the bank statements, could have assured him more of the sanity and security of Aaron's life.

It bothered Nick, when he thought about it. If Aaron was so good and so perfect, what was he doing with the likes of Nick? Here was a man who could finish a crossword in the time it took a kettle to boil; who could write a book on any subject he chose in the time that it would have taken Nick to read it. You couldn't point out a flower to him without him spouting Latin, while everyone else was still struggling to remember whether it was a daisy or a dandelion. He was a complete know-all, who was not ashamed of the fact. Nick was convinced, from one moment to the next, that Aaron was going to turn around and say that the whole affair had been nothing more than a bit of research into the underclasses. Nothing would have surprised him less.

Aaron, on the other hand, had nothing more than love as his excuse for being with Nick. To anyone who has never been in love, this is inexplicable. Love is a sort of fanaticism. It entails a belief which will override any evidence that the love is mistaken. The worst of Aaron's doubts had come to him in Mysore, when the physical distance between him and Nick had been greatest. Had their separation been a long one, the doubts might have had a chance to germinate, but they were unbearable to him and he came home to banish them. Now, in Nick's presence, any doubt that came didn't stand a chance of survival. Whenever Nick touched him, or looked at him, he had an overwhelming sense that it was right for them to be together. Anything which contradicted this was unacceptable. Ironically, it was Nick who, being familiar with addiction, was better equipped to deal with the anomalies and self-deception which love entailed.

The sight of the drinks cupboard was making Nick reckless, and he took an uncharacteristic gamble. 'Why do you love me?' he asked.

Aaron was putting whisky into tumblers that must have weighed half a pound each. 'What?'

'Why would someone like you fall in love with someone like me?'

'Don't put yourself down.' Despite his democratic notions Aaron assumed that Nick was referring to their social inequality.

'I'm not putting myself down. But we're hardly an even match.'

'Maybe. Maybe not. I don't know. Does it matter? You don't choose whom you fall in love with. I saw you and I fell in love with you. Before I knew who or what you were, every instinct I had told me that you were the man I was looking for. I fancied you something rotten, but there was more to it than that. Anyway, I've always trusted my instinct before, and it's usually been right, about the important things.'

'So you just love me because you think you have to be right about everything.'

'That's a horrible thing to say,' Aaron retorted, partly because there was some truth in it, and it was an accusation he'd had levelled at him before.

'So, bam. You fell in love and there was nothing you could do about it?'

'In some ways.'

'So you wouldn't love me if you had the choice?'

'I didn't say that. You're being perverse.'

Aaron was sitting on one of the sofas, looking at the pathetic mound of Nick's belongings on the floor. Nick sat beside him, but not touching. He had stuck his neck out, but not had enough answers yet for touching. After a lifetime of being involved with men whose motives were no better than his own, he seemed to have found one who was doing everything for the best reasons, but he wanted to be sure. Nick was thinking that, maybe, if Aaron was all he appeared to be, then it would be worthwhile to change, and become a good person too, but if the whole thing was a big con there was no point in being a sucker. He had been laughed at too many times to want to go through that again. He said, 'I want this to work.'

'So do I.' Aaron was speaking so seriously that it made Nick shake, the whisky slopping about in the tumbler. 'It will. I know it will.' Aaron's words were coming out singly, and leaden. 'I think we're more equal than you realise. I think we are both people who can get exactly what we want. There are few people I've met who are more determined to have their own way than you are. If we both want the same thing, there is no way that it can't happen.'

'So you love me because I'm stubborn?'

'I love you because I saw you. Your being stubborn makes it more likely to work. I know I'm right about this.'

'So you do always think you're right.'

'Mostly,' Aaron said, without hesitation.

'You're an arrogant bastard.'

'So?'

They were both smiling by now. Nick had had enough answers to be lying in Aaron's lap. Nick's glass was empty; Aaron's almost untouched. 'What if,' Nick asked, 'you found out something terrible about me?'

'Such as?'

'I don't know. Say I was a vampire or something?'

'I could deal with that.' Aaron looked at Nick in a clinical way, as though he expected the fangs to appear. 'Whatever you've done in the past, or whatever I've done, for that matter, was wiped clean the day we met. Now we can be who we really are, and not what we used to seem to be. Why are you crying?'

'Do you mean that?'

'I always mean everything.' Seeing Nick weep, Aaron remembered the question which had haunted him in Mysore. Nick was so vulnerable now that it was unlikely he would respond flippantly, and the question was so metaphysical that there could be no expectation of an answer. Aaron thought only to exorcise the question by asking it aloud. 'Who are you?'

He could not have foreseen the force of Nick's response. Nick howled as though he were being tortured, and the howl broke down to a weeping repetition of, 'Don't ask me that. Please don't ask me that.'

There was nothing Aaron could say, because he thought that Nick had gone mad, and he knew nothing that could be said to madmen.

When he was calmer, Nick began to speak, but without making any more sense. He had swallowed the whisky from Aaron's tumbler in a single gulp. 'It's all about hope,' he said. 'Hope. Don't ask me who I am. This is the best time I've ever had. The best chance. You came out of nowhere, like an angel with news, and you're the only one who ever saw the good in me. I always knew I was meant to be good, but no one ever gave me the chance. What chance have you of being good if your own parents hate you? I could be clean and saved. I could be at ease with myself. But don't ask me who I am. That's what I'm trying to get away from. Help me. I need help. Don't ask questions, just help me.'

'I will,' Aaron said, not understanding, but thinking that his own certainty was the best contribution he could make. 'I love you. You know that.'

That made Nick feel better, to know that his saviour wasn't

someone sitting on a cloud, but a real man, running fingers through Nick's hair and smelling of sex and Chanel.

'Do you think,' Nick asked, as soon as he thought the atmosphere had settled, 'we should plug the telly in down here or up in the bedroom?'

The next day Aaron woke with the feeling that his life was complete. Everything was accomplished and secured, and there was nothing left to be done but enjoy the life he had created. The hunger that had set him wandering across the world was gone, and the need that used to have him scanning the eyes of strange men was satisfied. He put his hand on Nick's bare backside, as though he were touching a talisman. The flesh beneath his palm and fingers was like a guarantee.

Nick, he knew, was not a morning person, and would not be thankful to be woken. It was tempting to lie there until he woke of his own accord, smelling the pall of his breath across the pillow, furtively stretching a forefinger until it reached the sphincter. That idea made Aaron taut with lust, desperate to fuck his lover, which was the one thing that had been denied him. He was becoming obsessed by this arsehole. He had studied it and eaten it and put his tongue inside it, had plugged it with each of his fingers in turn and dribbled his sperm on it, rubbed his dick against it, and pushed his luck at moments when it seemed that Nick was so turned on it could be slipped into without resistance. Someday, Nick would promise, they could do it, but not yet. Perhaps, Aaron thought as he moved his hand away, not everything had been accomplished, but at least there was still something to look forward to.

Quietly, he got out of bed and left the darkened room. There was plenty to occupy him while he waited for Nick to get up. The house had not been dusted in months. There were shopping lists to be made, and he had taken a piece of haddock out of the freezer the night before to make kedgeree for breakfast.

He wrapped the coffee grinder in a tea towel to dull the noise and kept the radio on so low that he could barely hear it himself. He would have liked to hoover but thought it best to leave that until Nick was awake. In the past he had always done the housework automatically and efficiently, as a way of keeping dirt at bay, and had never thought much about it. Now he found pleasure in it, because he was under the impression that he was doing it for Nick's sake; that he was being useful and not just being tidy.

The television sat in the corner of the sitting room, on top of a wooden chest. When Aaron caught sight of it that morning he sat on the arm of a chair and looked at the blank screen for twenty minutes. It appeared an alien thing among the rest of the furniture. He had argued against having it in the bedroom. He had slept with people who kept televisions in bedrooms and it had seemed to him a slovenly practice. If there had to be a television in the house, at least it should be in a public and not a private room.

Aaron came to two conclusions in those twenty minutes. The first was that he was being snobbish. Television was the chosen recreation of the vast majority of people. If he preferred to spend his idle evenings reading and listening to music, that was not something he could impose on Nick. If they were to live together there would have to be compromises. Some of his friends, who had put up with his tirades against television over the years, were going to tease him about acquiring a set, but he had always maintained that it was a sign of intelligence to be able to change his mind. At least now they wouldn't be able to bait him about appearing on it from time to time when he was so against it.

The second conclusion was that the compromise should work both ways. If Nick was going to show him how the other half lived, then he would show Nick what his half got up to. There were days of freedom ahead of them and a city full of distractions and experiences which Nick had never had. Nick had admitted, unashamedly, that he had never been to an art gallery or an opera or a play or a botanical garden. It was time, Aaron decided, that his mind was opened to the world of ideas.

By the time Nick woke the schedule for the day was set. Had it been proposed to him in advance, he might have thought of objections, but he was given no choice in the matter.

'This is how it's going to be,' Aaron said. 'We're going to live life to the full.'

'At least tell me where we're going.'

'You'll see when we get there.'

'I don't know what to wear.'

'What you've got on is fine.'

'I can't go out like this.' He was wearing the jeans he'd had on the day before and a double-cuffed shirt of Aaron's.

'Trust me,' Aaron said. 'You look fine for where we're going.'

Halfway there, Aaron succumbed to Nick's badgering and told him they were on their way to Robinson House.

'What's that?'

'A garden. You must have heard of it.'

'A garden? At this time of year? What's the point of that? We won't even be able to sit on the grass.'

'There are palm houses. You'll see. I go there all the time to sketch.'

Nick felt a twinge of embarrassment at the mention of

sketching. It was not an activity of which he thought it proper to speak aloud. 'I'm going to be bored,' he said. 'I know it.'

He was enchanted by Robinson House, once they were there. They were alone in the palm houses, it being a weekday and a slack time of year. 'It's just like India,' he kept saying. 'I never knew about this. Why doesn't everyone know about this? We should come here all the time. Can't we grow plants like this? Why don't we get a greenhouse? What's that one called?'

'I don't know.'

'Don't know? That's a big admission coming from you. I thought you knew everything.'

'It's probably a *Dicksonia*. Look at the label: *antartica* I should think.' Aaron was taking a chance in naming the only species of tree fern he was familiar with.

'It is. How did you know that?'

Aaron shrugged. He couldn't stop grinning at Nick's pleasure. He beamed and Nick bounced from plant to plant, stroking the banana leaves and asking questions to test him.

'You've asked me that one twice already. It's a camellia.'

'But it's a different colour from the last one.'

Aaron began to explain the basic principles of plant identification, but Nick was already sniffing the next flower and asking the next question.

On the way out of the gardens Nick found an enormous pine cone. 'I'm going to keep this,' he said, 'to remind me.'

Aaron looked about him to see if they were being watched. 'Strictly speaking you shouldn't. It's stealing.' Seeing the look of incomprehension on Nick's face he realised he was being a bit of a prude, and added, 'Better stick it under your coat so the man at the gate doesn't see.'

'Where next? Home?'

'There's a full day ahead yet. Lunch next.'

'Where? Somewhere glamorous hopefully.'

'You hope.'

'What?'

'Not hopefully. You hope. Never mind. We'll do semantics another day. The National Gallery.'

'That doesn't sound glamorous.'

'Wait and see.'

By the time they had finished lunch the edge had gone off Nick's excitement. 'Do we have to see these paintings?' he asked. 'I'm tired.'

'We should, as we're here. The exhibition finishes next week. I thought I was going to miss it altogether, what with being away and all.'

'Does that mean you came back for the paintings and not for me?'

'Of course not.' Aaron was shocked by the suggestion.

'Joke, Aaron. It was a joke. Remember those? At least let's have another bottle of wine to keep us going.'

Aaron made a face. They had got through two bottles already.

'Well I'm ordering one anyway.' He called the waiter over and asked for the wine, and a large brandy as well. 'It's not often I get taken out to lunch. I wish you'd told me we were coming somewhere like this. I'm dressed like a tramp.'

'So am I.'

'That doesn't make it any better. You culture vultures have no idea, do you? The best dressed people in here are the waiters.'

Aaron began to show signs of impatience while the brandy and the wine were being finished.

'What's the matter?' Nick asked.

'Nothing.'

'Well stop drumming your fingers on the table then. Just talk to me. Am I boring you?'

'Of course not.'

'I know I am. I know what this is all about. I've seen *My Fair Lady*. Eight times. I know you want to educate me so I'm not an embarrassment to you.'

'I'm unembarrassable. Anyway, that isn't what I'm doing. I wanted to show you some of the things I liked. I thought you'd be interested.'

'Well I am. I loved that garden thing, Robinson whatever it was. Just don't expect everything at once.'

The exhibition, which was of nineteenth century Spanish masters, did not appeal to Nick. He yawned in front of a late Goya, which had Aaron bristling with indignation, though nothing was said. Nick took more interest in the activities of the other spectators.

'The amount of cruising that's going on in here. I've never seen anything like it. It's like a knocking shop.'

'Where?'

'Everywhere. The place is crawling with trade. And rent. Look, that one over there, with the mobile phone. I recognise him. He's a friend of Paul's. Back in a minute.'

Nick went over to the youth he had indicated and they both walked off in the direction of the lavatories. Aaron found himself standing alone in front of a painting of three lemons, unable to focus. There was such a dread in him that his faculties almost ceased to function. What was Nick doing? Why had he gone to the lavatory with someone he had identified as a prostitute? Aaron didn't know what to do. Should he wait, or should he follow them? If he did follow them, what was he likely to find? He had just decided that it was better to know the worst, when he saw Nick coming towards him, looking pleased with himself

'Scored.'

'What?'

'Fabrice does a little dealing on the side. I've scored an eighth. I'm beginning to see the point of this culture business. I didn't think anyone would come all this way to see a few splodgy old paintings.'

'Some people do.'

'Oh come on. Any of the good ones you can buy as birthday cards. You don't have to stand around in a gallery and pretend to be all soulful.'

One all, Aaron thought. Let's see who gets the best out of three.

'Can we go home now? I've had enough improvement for one day.'

'I thought we'd go to the cinema.'

Originally, Aaron had thought that they would go to the opera. There was a Puccini on that night, which would have been a safe introduction, he judged. As it would have been impossible to book at such late notice, going would have involved hanging around until the bell, in the hope of buying returned tickets. He could now see that Nick might be difficult to handle under those circumstances. He had a second plan. The Kieslowski trilogy was being shown in the centre of town, and *Blue* was starting at six.

'Oh good. I want to see that Keanu Reeves thing.'

'What Keanu Reeves thing?'

'You know, the one that's on. I can't remember the name. Who cares anyway, so long as Keanu's in it.'

'I thought we'd see *Three Colours Blue*.'

'Never heard of it.'

'It's very good. I think you'll like it.'

'Great. We've been doing what you want all day. Isn't it time we did something I want?'

'Just try it.'

'Anything for a sit-down I suppose. I want a drink first. All this art stuff is making me thirsty.'

Nick was deeply affected by the first twenty-five minutes of the film. He wept loudly and clutched Aaron's hand. Though he was made uncomfortable by such a public display of emotion, Aaron took this to mean that the film had been a good choice. The exhibition had been a washout, but Aaron couldn't fault Nick on the honesty of his reactions. The paintings had bored him and he had said so. Nick's enthusiasm for the palm houses and the film had made the day worthwhile. It had been hard work, but satisfying.

Just as Aaron was congratulating himself, Nick said that he needed to go to the Gents. He was gone about fifteen minutes. When he came back he seemed to have lost interest in the film, and fell asleep for the rest of it. There was a faint smell of marijuana about him.

The proof that the day had been a success came later. Nick insisted that they stop at the Twisted Arms for a drink on the way home. There were a few people in, and all at the same table. Nick dominated the conversation, holding forth on what a fantastic day he'd had, showing off his new knowledge like a boy back from his first scout camp.

Ed, laughing up his sleeve, threw Aaron a cynical look. 'You'll have him writing poetry next,' he said.

The idea to write a book of recipes for chicken breasts came to Aaron in the supermarket. Though, for the most part, his perceptions were occluded by love, his commercial sense had remained intact and he could still recognise a moneyspinner when it was staring at him from the meat cabinets. There were yards and tiers of chicken breasts, outnumbering all the other portions of animal put together. Aaron had never been tempted to buy a chicken breast himself, being the sort of person who, if such a thing were called for, would take a whole chicken and dismantle it, make stock of the bones and a separate dish of the spare flesh. That was why it struck him as remarkable that enormous numbers of people, lacking in either time or imagination, were paying over the odds for what was, to him, the least interesting part of the fowl. He hovered about for a while to see who was buying the things. As he suspected, it was the younger, fitter, wealthier class of customer: exactly the sort of person who would also fork out for an overdesigned cookery book. By the time he was through the checkout the book was complete in his head, save for a catchy title. The one drawback he could see in the project was that he and Nick would be sick of eating chicken breast before he had tested half of the recipes. He consoled himself that Nick didn't seem to mind or notice what he ate in any case, as long as there was a bottle of ketchup on the table.

While Aaron was out, Nick was making the best of the time he had to himself. He had just settled down to watch *Home And Away*, when he heard the sound of keys in the hall. 'That was quick darling,' he called out. 'What did you get me?'

A woman's voice replied, 'Who the hell are you?'

She was standing by the door, doing her best to look menacing, and poised for flight at the same time, in case the person on the sofa should turn out to be something she couldn't handle. Nick knew, the moment he saw her, that she had to be related to Aaron. She had the same teeth, the same inflection in her voice and the same way of holding her tallness; long from the hips down and leaning back from the waist up.

'Nick,' he answered. 'Who are you?'

'What are you doing here?' She didn't say that she was going to call the police, but it was implicit in her voice.

'I'm with Aaron. He's back.'

'Where is he?'

'Sainsbury's.'

She gave the room the once-over, as if checking for squatter's graffiti, and then settled a hard stare on Nick. He had not been long out of bed and wasn't looking his best. There was a full ashtray and a vodka bottle and a pornographic magazine on the table in front of him. He had been planning a wank before *Neighbours*, since it was the first time he'd been left in the house alone since Sunday night, and he was bored with quickies over the bathroom sink and furtive ejaculations into a sock under the bedclothes while Aaron made breakfast in the mornings. He wanted to be able to spread his legs and stick his middle finger up his bottom and have a good long fantasy about Gregor, the Latvian hunk on pages thirty-four, thirty-five and thirty-seven.

Now Gregor would have to be postponed. Nick covered the porn with a copy of *Hello!* before the intruder had a chance to see exactly what it was.

Once he'd persuaded the woman that he wasn't dangerous, she went off to check the rest of the house and find evidence that her brother really had returned from his travels, which gave Nick the chance to stash the vodka and the dodgy magazine. She was still wary when she returned, but Nick took no notice, and chatted amiably with one eye on the screen. It turned out that she knew India well, having been several times, so Nick was able to hold forth, telling her several things which she could have told him better, had she been able to get a word in. When *Neighbours* came on he was on more solid ground, giving her insights into the characters and a list of reasons why Brad's legs were the best thing on television.

Though she had an appointment to go to, she was not prepared to leave until she had seen Aaron, and refused to sit down in the meantime, constantly keeping a clear run between herself and the door. It was clear that Aaron was back (there was fresh houmous in the fridge and Aaron was the only person she knew who bothered to make his own) and that Nick was acquainted with him, but otherwise the situation was inexplicable to her. She had not been in favour of the whole travel business from the beginning, or 'dropping out', as she had called it. 'You can't just abandon your life and expect to pick it up again a year later,' she had said. He had answered, 'Perhaps I won't want to.'

'Well, what do you want?'

'That's what I'm going to find out. I've got all the things that people are supposed to want. What do you expect me to do now? Grow old and complacent?'

'That's a very selfish attitude.'

'No,' he had said, so quietly that she knew he meant it. 'This is about not becoming some kind of selfish monstrosity.

You have the children to think about. You have a biological reason not to become selfish. All I can think about is what colour to paint the sitting room next. The only solution I can think of is to go and lose myself for a while.'

'And what is that supposed to achieve? What's the point?'

'There isn't one. That is exactly why it has to be done.'

She hadn't understood, but was prepared to give him the benefit of the doubt. Now he had returned, early, and with the sort of creature who would have you hailing a taxi if you found yourself sharing a bus shelter with him. Bracing herself for the worst, she would stay put until she had had an explanation.

When Aaron arrived she greeted him with an air of accusation. He was simmering with excitement at his chicken breast scheme, and naively pleased by the sight of his sister.

'I was going to phone you. We just wanted a few days on our own first, before we told anyone we were back.' He was sitting on the arm of the sofa, stroking the back of Nick's head. 'I hadn't realised you'd be calling in.'

'Twice a week,' she said. 'Like you asked me to.'

'Sorry. There hasn't been time to think.' He looked at Nick, as if the half-dressed man with bleary eyes should explain his distraction.

'I would have thought,' she said, 'that you'd be desperate to see Hu, if no one else.'

Nick stiffened at the mention of what sounded like another man's name. 'Who's that?' he asked, indignantly.

'My cat,' Aaron said, sounding to Nick as though he had been caught out. 'I told you about Hu. Susan's been minding him for me.'

'Yes,' Nick said, in the triumphant tone of someone who hasn't been fooled that easily. 'You told me you had a cat, but it was called something else.'

'Hubris. Hu for short.'

Nick wasn't convinced, but he said no more, thinking that he would have a better chance of getting the truth out of Aaron later, when they were alone.

'We'll come round and pick him up tonight,' Aaron said. 'Then Nick can meet Simon and the children.'

Susan looked at her brother as though he had just suggested a gang-bang in the high street, but since she couldn't think of a plausible way of getting out of it, she said, 'About seven,' through clenched teeth. At least, she reasoned, the children would be safely in bed.

'No,' Nick said. 'We'll miss Corrie.'

The others looked at him with blank expressions. Susan asked Aaron who Corrie was, and Aaron had to ask Nick.

'What planet do you people live on?' Nick demanded, as patiently as he could manage. '*Coronation Street*.'

'Do you watch all the soaps?' Susan enquired, in the sort of regal voice that is mainly channelled down the nose.

'No,' Nick said, feeling cornered. He couldn't tell whether Aaron was smiling to cover embarrassment or siding with his sister in condescension. 'Corrie's the only one I'm bothered about.' He then remembered the expertise he had shown on the subject of *Neighbours*, and added, 'And sometimes the Australian ones, if I've nothing better to do.'

Aaron came to his rescue and distracted Susan by asking her what had been happening in *The Archers* while he'd been away, and they spent ten minutes assassinating the character of Susan Carter, unfairly, Nick thought, since her worst crime seemed to have been a penchant for reproduction Georgian doors.

This burst of normal conversation reminded Susan that she had a life to get on with, and she left in a hurry, saying that she was going to be late for a brief.

'What's a brief?' Nick asked, when she had gone.

'She's a barrister. She and Simon both. They met while defending the Costello Street strangler.'

'Scum like that should be strung up, not defended.'

Aaron thought about explaining the principle of justice for all, but he checked himself. It was hard to believe that Nick had meant what he had said. It might have been said ironically, and Aaron was afraid of offending Nick by accusing him of such a base and tabloid sentiment. He was even more afraid, perhaps, of discovering that Nick was a serious advocate of lynching; that he had fallen in love with a man with a hateful mind.

It was nothing short of perverse then that Aaron, when he could easily have talked about chicken breasts, chose instead to ask Nick why he had lied about watching the soaps.

'I wasn't going to have your sister think that I was the sort of person who spends his life in front of a television.'

'But you are.'

'That's not fair.'

'I'd rather,' Aaron explained, 'have her think you were a soap addict than let her know that you are a compulsive liar.'

'Is that what you think of me?'

'I may be in love, but I'm not stupid.'

Nick couldn't understand why these things were being said so calmly, why they weren't fighting by now. Aaron was talking in a measured, affectionate voice, and Nick was infected with an overwhelming fear; a dread that Aaron was able to see him for what he really was.

Aaron continued, 'I do notice that, given a choice, you always lie, even about the most trivial things.'

'Do you think I lie to you?' Nick was shaking by this stage. This was the sort of talk that might signal the end of everything.

'Not about the big things. I think you love me too much to take that risk.'

'So that's it then? You don't trust me?'

Aaron said all sorts of things to get out of that one. He said that he trusted himself. He said that he believed in Nick. He said that lying was only a habit that Nick had fallen into because he wasn't at ease with himself; that if he could show Nick the man he was in love with, then Nick would have the confidence never to lie again. Lies, he said, were nothing more than a symptom of something which could be cured by love.

Nick had never, in his entire life, felt so exposed or ashamed of himself. He had his head on Aaron's chest so that his face couldn't be seen. He had been stripped of an elaborate shell and left slimy, like the mollusc beneath. Unable to fight without armour, he had no choice but to make an attempt at explaining himself. A drink would have made it easier, but he was too afraid to ask for one. Each word came away from him in pain, like gouged lumps of his flesh flung across the room.

'I'm not exactly proud of what I am. You can't understand, because you've made something of your life. You don't know how proud I am of you. You've got a brain. I see this house and all the books with your name on the cover, and the others you've written as well, and I hear the way you talk, and it doesn't just make me proud of you. It makes me ashamed of myself. I'm used to being around people who are more like me. And the nicer you are to me the more worthless I feel. I can't help it. I saw the way your sister was looking at me, and I wasn't even dressed properly. She didn't think I was good enough for you. And it'll be the same with the rest of your friends. How are you going to introduce me? "This is my boyfriend. He may be on the dole but he never misses Brooky. Go on, ask him anything about the Close." I'm not qualified for anything. The only time I get to wear a suit is at funerals, and then I have to borrow one. There's nothing I could do with my life that would make your friends think I was the right sort of person for you. Maybe I do lie a bit sometimes, but it's the only shred of dignity I can have, and you'll never understand that because you're lucky and you don't need to lie. People respect you for what you are. Go on, you can hit me if you like. I know you want to. I've let you down.'

Aaron had been listening in a daze. The offer of violent retribution brought him crashing back to reality.

'Don't say that,' he said. 'I couldn't hit you. How could I hit you?'

'That's how it usually ends. Why should you be any different. Don't worry. I can give as good as I get.'

'It's me, Nick. Me. I don't know who you've been with in the past, but this is me. I am different from that. I've never hit anyone in my life.'

'That's what they all say. To begin with. Everyone's the same. I'll bring the devils out in you before you can find the angel in me.'

'No,' Aaron said. 'If I know anything, I know it will never come to that. I love you.'

'Love can't change the way we're made. We're men. Things get nasty.'

Nick was half asleep as he was speaking, exhausted by the afternoon's high emotion. Aaron let him drop off, and then slid out from beneath him, to put the shopping away. He worked quietly in the kitchen for a while, before going upstairs to his office to put the chicken breast scheme on the computer.

When Aaron returned, the repeat of *Neighbours* was on the television and Nick was watching it.

'I've been thinking,' Aaron began.

'Shush. It's *Neighbours*. I missed most of this because of your sister.' Nick sounded a little drunk, but Aaron thought that was understandable, in the circumstances.

When the soap was over, Aaron began again. 'I was

thinking, about what you were saying. About me being lucky and you needing to do something.'

'Can't we just leave it now? Can't we just forget I said anything? I don't think I can stand any more little lectures about self-esteem. Why don't you just write a book about it if you're so interested? I'm not.'

Aaron had, in fact, once written something called, *The Inner You: 100 Ways To Nurture*. It had been intended as a spoof on the self-help industry, but since this wasn't mentioned on the jacket, the book was taken seriously. It sold particularly well in New Zealand, in a pirated edition, unfortunately. Now was not the moment to mention it.

'I was thinking along more practical lines,' Aaron said. 'What about that nightclub you were planning to open? The big project you had to get home for?'

The whole nightclub business had, in fact, been one of Nick's more elaborate lies, told to Aaron at a time when Nick, though in a welter of emotion, didn't seriously expect the relationship to last more than a week. Aaron had been due to move on to the next stage of his travels. If he turned out to be no more than a holiday shag and, in Nick's experience, that was the most realistic expectation, no harm would have been done by the fabrication. On the other hand, if the relationship worked out he had plenty of time to come up with a covering story. It had not been a difficult invention. Nick and his friends often had a fantasy game about the sort of club they would open, if they could. In his efforts to impress Aaron, impresario had a better ring to it than unemployed busboy. Now, Nick hoped that if he was vague enough about the details, the whole thing would be forgotten. As far as he could tell, Aaron was rich enough for both of them.

'I told you,' Nick said. 'The finance fell through. These things aren't that easy to get off the ground you know.'

'I'll help.'

'That isn't the point. You don't know anything about the business. I do.' Nick was irritated by the blind optimism with which Aaron approached everything. You couldn't just say no to Aaron. He always wanted to know the reason why not and was then more than likely to suggest a solution. It made covering his tracks a tiresome business.

'Well think about it. I wasn't born lucky. I made this life. I didn't find it.'

'Well you're not me.'

'And I'm not any better than you. You can do anything you want. I believe in you. There's no reason why you shouldn't believe in yourself.'

'Hallelujah. Amen, brother.' Dropping the sarcasm, Nick added, 'In that case maybe you should leave me to do it myself. There's no point in making something of myself if you can take all the credit. Maybe you should just trust me.'

There was nothing more Aaron could say. He had a nagging feeling that he had just suffered some kind of defeat. When the time came for him to go to Susan's and collect the cat, Nick refused to go with him, saying that he had had enough of being sneered at for one day.

The cat, once it was back, hit it off with Nick straight away. They had a lot in common, Nick and Hu, needing little more than a comfortable sofa in front of the telly and the attentions of the right kind of man. Aaron looked at the two of them curled up together and said, 'You see, you must be a good person, if animals take to you like that. Hu doesn't put himself out for just anyone.'

Somehow, like pulling a face when the wind changes and being stuck with it, there is a danger that someday a declaration of love will be made just as the breeze is shifting, and there is no way back to normality. Not that Aaron had any idea yet of the distortion he had got himself into. Nothing, in his view, was insuperable.

Susan, on the other hand, believed that she had cause for concern. At the first red light she came to after leaving Aaron's house that day she got out her mobile phone and called Brian Yeats.

'Aaron's back,' she said, cutting short the usual effusion of his greeting.

'He can't be. When? I thought he was going to stay away for a year.'

'He's back.'

'Susan? Is something the matter? He's not ill or anything?'

'No. Nothing as simple as that. I think he might need our help though.'

'Where is he? At home? For God's sake Susan, you've got me worried. What's up?'

'Oh probably nothing,' she said. She realised that she should have worked out what to say before phoning. She didn't like using the phone and driving at the same time, but she was late for work and couldn't pull over. It was hard not to sound flustered. In her professional life she was known for her calm, but it wasn't possible to be so controlled where her brother was concerned. 'He's got himself involved with someone.'

'What someone? Who is this person?'

'Someone called Nick. You'd have to see him Brian, to know what I'm talking about. He's an airhead. He's psychotic. Aaron's completely spellbound by him. You know how Aaron's always taking on lame ducks?'

'Yes?' Brian answered doubtfully. His friendship with Aaron having begun romantically, he didn't like to hear himself described as a lame duck. 'Don't you think Aaron is capable of looking after himself? How awful can this man be?'

'You don't understand. I know what I'm talking about. I come across people like Nick all the time. In the courts. If we don't do something, that man is going to kill my brother.'

'I'm sorry Susan, but I have to say that sounds a little melodramatic.'

'All right. You'll just have to see for yourself. That's why I'm calling you. Aaron's coming over to my house at seven to pick up Hu. Can you make it?'

'Is this Nick going to be there?'

'I don't know. Apparently it might interfere with *Coronation Street*.'

'That's understandable. Raquel is having a terrible time at the moment.'

'Who's Raquel?'

'Calm down, Susan. That was a joke. Of course I'll be there.'

So when Aaron arrived to pick up the cat, he found Brian sitting at his sister's kitchen table with Simon, and a bottle of red wine between them.

Brian was one of those comfortable men, a little old before

his time, but content to be so. He wore clothes that other people chose for him and had his hair cut whenever it began to interfere with his vision. He was big and graceless and the kind of friend you'd be most likely to phone if you were in trouble. He looked like a general practitioner, which, in fact, he was. The physical part of his relationship with Aaron had lasted a week, ten years previously, and had been so unremarkable that neither of them could remember much about it. A strong friendship had grown up in its stead.

Though Susan had told him that Aaron was a changed man, he had chosen to dismiss most of her account as neurotic exaggeration. She was a frighteningly capable person when events were within her control, but had a tendency to panic in the face of the unknown. Brian had come along to see his friend, not to be part of Susan's crusade.

Now, he had to admit, she had a point. Something was gone in Aaron, as though he were under hypnosis, though it would have taken a close friend to spot it. He was not quite the urbane, cynical, quick-witted man who had set off round the world a few months before. Aaron was thinner also, which was hardly surprising considering the countries he had been travelling through, but it made his tallness almost comical, like a gangly skeleton rattling about the kitchen. He wore a permanent, stupid grin, as though he were on a high dose of librium, in place of the once devastating, humorous smile. It was his eyes, however, which showed the greatest difference. They were like the eyes of an addict, at once glazed and unnaturally bright, as though they saw nothing in the material world before him, but were fixed on something illusory and more demanding. His voice was dead, though it spoke of knowing what it was to be really alive.

Susan stayed out of the way, and called Simon up to say goodnight to the children. She wanted Brian and Aaron to be left alone.

'So what's he like?' Brian thought he might as well go straight to the heart of things.

'Nick? Susan's been telling you about that, has she?'

'She said you'd found someone.'

'I'm in love, Brian.'

'So I can see.'

'Is it that obvious?'

'You're not exactly yourself. Who's the lucky man?'

'Nick Lovely. Isn't that a fantastic name?'

'And is he? Lovely?'

'Yes.' Aaron drew the word out into a sigh of illustration.

'What does he do then?' Brian was trying not to sound sharp.

Aaron could see the problems Nick had when faced with the same question. He found himself paraphrasing Nick's prevarications. 'It's something to do with nightclubs. He used to work at Priapus, but now he's setting up on his own. He was a pop star in the eighties.'

'I've never heard of him.' Thinking that sounded too cynical, Brian added, 'But then I don't know who any of these people are. I had to get someone to explain Michael Jackson to me the other day. Hum one of his songs. Perhaps I'll recognise that.'

Aaron didn't like to admit that he had never heard any musical evidence of Nick's early career. 'Oh it was all that New Romantic stuff,' he said. 'You know the kind of thing.'

'All those blokes with fringes?'

'Yes. Exactly.'

'So are you back now, or are you going away again?'

'Oh I'm back. I'm definitely back. Travelling's all very well for the single. I've got responsibilities now.'

'Like what?'

'Like a man to look after.' Brian looked at him so oddly that Aaron added, 'He can't boil an egg. Someone has to keep him out of the pizza parlours.'

'You don't have that much in common then?'

The fact that he was being interrogated finally got through to Aaron. 'What is this?' he asked. 'Has Susan been saying something? Is that why you're here?'

Brian denied it, and claimed that he'd called round earlier, by chance. He didn't want Aaron to become paranoid. Things looked bad enough without Aaron feeling that his friends were out to get him. At that moment there was a clattering by the back door and Hu came strolling through the cat flap. He jumped straight onto Aaron's lap, closed his eyes and began to treadle and dribble in ecstasy.

'She just said she was a bit worried, that's all. What with your coming back early and not telling anyone.'

'I'm fine,' Aaron said. 'I've never been better. I've never been happier. Just because Nick doesn't belong to the same world as you or I doesn't mean that he's bad for me. If anything, it's going to be harder for him to adjust. I've already met most of his friends. They're a bit of a mixed bunch, but that goes to show how open-minded he is. He's made me realise that you can't spend your whole life in some kind of middle class ivory tower. People like us think we've got all the answers, but the fact is that we don't even know what the problems are.'

'I think,' Brian said in an offended tone, 'I can say that I see a fair share of the world's problems in my surgery.'

'Sorry, I didn't mean you.'

'Who did you mean?'

'I meant me. I'm seeing life; raw, exciting life. Apart from being in love and having found the man I want to spend the rest of my days with. I feel as though I'm beginning to understand why the world is the way it is: why people are angry and why they watch soap operas and why no one reads novels any more.'

'I do.'

'That isn't relevant. You know exactly what I mean. Nick

isn't just the man I love. He's all the things we always droned on about and never took responsibility for. When I went away I didn't know what I was looking for, but now that I've found Nick I know it was him. You have to meet him, Brian. You'd like him. I know you would.'

Aaron didn't stay long after that. He was on his feet and restless, with Hu furling round his ankles and tripping him up. All the talk of Nick had given him something like a pain, though where it was located he couldn't have said. He only knew that the pain would be relieved the moment Nick laid a hand on him. He was, whether he knew it or not, expecting miracles of love.

The door had barely closed behind him before Brian was being grilled by Susan.

'I was right, wasn't I?'

'About what? He seems smitten enough.' Brian knew that nothing would be achieved by fuelling Susan's prejudice.

'Something has to be done.'

'Like what? He's not a teenager who's run off with the Moonies. People fall in love all the time. As often as not it ends badly, I admit, but there's nothing you can do to prevent it.'

'That's easy for you to say. You haven't met this Nick creature.'

'Exactly. And you've only met him once, and under trying circumstances, from what I understand. Aaron knows him better than any of us and I, for one, trust his judgement. If Aaron loves the man I am prepared to think that the man is worthy of it. And if Aaron has made a mistake, I know for a fact that he is intelligent enough to realise it once the novelty has worn off. I know he's your baby brother, but he has grown up.'

'Not much, judging by this,' she said. 'Fat lot of help you are.'

There was some excitement in the new household on Saturday. Nick and Aaron would be going to Priapus together for the first time. Going out was a serious business for Nick, and a lot of preparation was involved. Aaron was entranced by how much time and effort a man could invest for an appearance in a dark, sweaty club where most of the other patrons would have taken enough Ecstasy to make a doorpost seem attractive. The afternoon was set aside for eyelash tinting, for which Nick had to spend a long time lying on his back in the middle of the floor with bits of tissue paper stuck to his face.

'Is it worth the trouble?' Aaron asked.

'Trouble? This is nothing. There was a time when I used to dye everything. And I mean everything. Arsehairs, the lot. I wanted people to think I was Italian. Dark looks were fashionable then.'

Aaron tried to imagine it. He decided that it couldn't have been very convincing, with Nick's freckled, papery skin.

Nick emerged from the eyelash tint looking as though he was wearing brown mascara. It was not, Aaron judged, an improvement. This was followed by an hour and a half of close shaving, ear, nose and eyebrow trimming and Aaron being called on to shave the back of his neck. Nick not only put wax on his hair, but squirted a fat cloud of hairspray over that. Aaron was about to say that the whole point of having extremely short hair like Nick's was that it didn't need that kind of maintenance, but he was beginning to work out that he was observing a ritual which he shouldn't interfere in, so he kept his opinions to himself. Preparation H was applied round the eyes to tighten the skin. The effect, together with the browned eyelashes, was a sort of stary Barbie doll look. Aaron was beginning to realise how he had failed to recognise Nick from his previous appearances at Priapus. Getting dressed should have been simple. No one but the most outrageously vain label addicts wore anything but a T-shirt and jeans or, in any case, nothing that couldn't be put in a boil-wash afterwards to remove inexplicable stains. Nick however, managed, in an increasingly bad temper, to try on every pair of jeans he possessed, and several of Aaron's (which were far too tight on him and six inches too long in the leg), before he was satisfied. Even then he suffered a last minute crisis. 'Do these jeans make me look fat?'

'No.' Aaron wasn't lying. It was the fat which made Nick look fat.

'You're just saying that. I know they make me look fat. Why have I got so fucking fat? I used to have a nice body.'

'You look fine.' Aaron wasn't even tempted to point out that sitting in front of the television all day with a can of lager in your hand had yet to make anyone thinner.

'I'm going to start taking speed next week. I can't bear looking like this. I hate myself. You must be so ashamed to be going out with me. T-shirt in, or out?'

'In?'

'No. Out. I've got to hide this stomach somehow.'

Then there were the boots, which had to be levered on with a lot of grunting and red-faced straining. This was too much for Aaron. He hated to see anyone in pain. 'Can't you wear a pair that fits?'

'These do fit. Once I've got them on. They don't hurt that much. I can't go out looking like I've got big feet.'

'Why not?'

Nick gave Aaron a shrivelling look and said, 'Just help me get the fucking things on.'

All of this was done to the sound of disco anthems of the previous twenty years, played at full volume. When Nick was finally happy with his transformation (Aaron thought he'd looked better before, but didn't dare to say so), he turned his attention on Aaron.

'What are you wearing?'

'This. I changed while you were in the bathroom.'

'You can't go out like that.'

'Why not?' Aaron looked down at his black jeans and blue T-shirt. They seemed appropriate.

'Blue and black. Nobody wears blue and black. I'm not having people laugh at us.'

Aaron was stunned. He had always been considered an elegant dresser. Now, it seemed there was some sartorial rule he'd never heard of, and he was transgressing it. Meekly, he changed his T-shirt for a white one.

'That's better,' Nick said. 'A bit scruffy, but you'll do.'

The Twisted Arms came next. In the past Aaron had always gone to Priapus with one or two friends. Now he found himself part of a large posse of clubbers, some of whom he recognised from India. Cathy was there, but she pretended to take no notice of him, which was easy, since the crowd was so thick that you had to stand on one leg and move sideways. Nick sparkled; laughing loudly and gulping down drink. 'I've never gone to a club sober yet,' he said. Aaron had to stop himself thinking about the implications of this slightly boastful observation.

Outside the club, Nick tapped Elvira on the shoulder. He had made his arrangements in advance this time, so he could afford to be more perfunctory. 'Martin's list. Nick, plus one. There it is. I can see it.'

Elvira scanned the length of Aaron, and said to Nick, 'I heard you were going up in the world. Does he pack flat or do you have to roll him up when you're not using him?' He handed the guest passes to Aaron, saying, 'Whatever he's charging you, love, it's too much. Everyone else had it for free.'

'Do you know him then?' Aaron asked when they were through.

'Elvira? Everyone knows Elvira. That's why he's there.'

It was the time when ketamine was all the rage. Aaron had never taken it before, and probably wouldn't have taken it then if he'd known what it was, but he was sent to the bar and it was Nick who went to the dealer. Aaron swallowed what he was given, assuming that it was E. He had a strong reaction, and couldn't remember much about the first few hours, except that people were walking him up and down and slapping his face and tilting him over every time the vomit came dribbling out. The only thing he could think of was that he'd had a dog once who got distemper, and the symptoms, just before she died, had been more or less the same.

By the time Aaron was fit to dance, Nick announced that he was exhausted and they went to sit in the cafe. Nick was talking, but it was impossible to make out anything he said. The word love came into it a lot. Then a thuggish little man came up to them and grabbed Nick by the collar, and started going on about money, saying that Nick would have his legs broken if he didn't pay up. Nick went white and speechless, and it was a while after the man had gone before either of them could say anything.

'Who was that?' Aaron asked.

'John. He's just an ex-boyfriend.'

'So what was all that about?'

'He thinks I owe him three hundred quid.'

'Do you?'

'Oh for fuck's sake, don't you start as well. I want to go and dance. I want to forget all that.'

Because of the ketamine, it wasn't so much a dance as a token shuffle, with a lot of sweaty hugging when balance seemed out of the question. It was centuries before the music stopped and the lights came up.

Aaron had noticed that Nick didn't buy much drink, but whenever he saw an unattended lager can he would pick it up and shake it. If there was anything inside he'd hang on to it. Seeing the look on Aaron's face when he had done this for the third time, he defended himself by saying, 'It's only fair. I've had my drink stolen often enough. I'm just evening the score.' There was a flaw somewhere in that argument, and Aaron might have spotted it if his head hadn't been full of horse-tranquilliser.

Sunday morning went by with the curtains drawn. There was a lot of dribble on the pillows, and a lot of clinging together, like a couple who would not have been dismayed to find they had been transformed into Siamese twins. Aaron was woken at one point by the sound of Nick sobbing, and asked what was upsetting him.

'It's John. He means it. I know that bastard. And he knows the sort of people who would break my legs. For fifty quid.'

'Come on,' Aaron said. 'It's not going to happen. I'll give you the money.'

'Why are you so good to me all the time?'

'I can't see any reason for life to be so grim.' Aaron tried to think of cheerful things they could do for the day. He remembered the naive pleasure of their morning at Robinson House. 'We'll go to the palm houses this afternoon, shall we?'

'We've done that,' Nick snapped. 'I'm not going to

spend the rest of my life poncing round gardens while you show off your Latin. If we're going anywhere it's down to the Twisted. You can't have your own way all the time.'

'Anyone can make a mistake. Come on. If God hadn't made the fundamental mistake, none of us would be here to blame him for it.'

'It's a bit early in the morning for theology, Brian. What are you trying to say?'

'It's half past two in the afternoon. I dunno. I was just calling to see how you were.'

'I'm fine.'

'But you can't remember seeing me last night?'

'No.'

'What were you on?'

'Special K.'

'Are you out of your mind? Do you know what that stuff is?'

'I know I won't be doing it again. As you said, anyone can make a mistake.'

'Maybe, but it's not like you to admit it.' Brian was worried. He had seen Aaron and Nick at Priapus the night before. Both of them had been completely off their heads, but it wasn't that which concerned him. He'd taken an E himself. As a doctor, he was a realist where drugs were concerned. His unease had no specific grounds, but had something to do with the way that Aaron had given the impression of being unaware of anything but Nick. They had only met and spoken for a few seconds, and Aaron had treated him as though he were a stranger. In the past, if they had met in the same circumstances, they would have been inseparable for the rest of the evening. Now, Aaron couldn't even remember his being there.

'What's that supposed to mean?'

'Well, you do have a tendency to think yourself right all the time. Even when I prove you wrong, you still argue for the righteousness of your opinion.'

'Sorry Brian, I hadn't looked in my diary. I should have known that this was Phone Your Best Friend And Criticise Him For No Reason He Can Think Of Day. Is there a point to this?'

Brian was at a loss. What could he say? That he had been watching Nick in the club and didn't like the way the man operated? 'Sorry. I was just wondering about you and Nick. Whether you had any plans?'

'You mean apart from spending the rest of our lives together?'

'No, that's what I did mean. I wondered if you shouldn't be taking things a bit more slowly.'

'We are.'

'Just remember I'm here if you need me.'

'Why should I need you?'

'Thanks.'

'I didn't mean it like that. What I meant was everything is fine. I've never been so happy in my life. Nick is exactly what I've always needed.'

'Is he there now?'

'He's in bed. We both were. I'd just come down to the kitchen for a second when you called. Look, I don't know what you're so worried about, but you've got to stop. Why don't you come over and meet him. Lunch? Next Saturday?'

After he had put the phone down Aaron stood in front

of the open fridge for a long time, trying to remember what it was he had come downstairs for. Brian was such an old mother figure. Anyone would think that Nick was some kind of monster the way he was going on.

'This is all just snobbery,' Aaron said aloud. He should have foreseen this. People would take Nick for a bit of rough. He abandoned the fridge and went upstairs.

'I love you.'

'Why are you saying that now?'

'Because I think that if I love you enough anything is achievable.'

'Who was that on the phone?'

'Brian.'

'What did he want?'

'He saw us last night, apparently.'

'You should have pointed him out to me. Has he been upsetting you? Where's the tea?'

'I forgot.'

Later, when the tea was growing cold on the bedside table, Nick said, 'It's easy for you to talk about life not needing to be so grim. If I'd had your life I might think the same. You haven't done anything you're ashamed of.'

'Don't be too sure,' Aaron said, not thinking of any incident in particular, but on the generally accepted principle that everyone has something dreadful in their past.

'What? What did you do then? Fuck your ponies?' Nick laughed. 'Did you have to use a stool or did you train them to kneel down?'

'Generally, I let them get on top,' Aaron said, running with the joke.

'It's like millionaires who complain about having money worries,' Nick said, when they'd stopped sniggering. 'Everyone has to play the victim and get their five minutes on Oprah. People like you should just be grateful not to be people like me.'

'Happiness,' Aaron said, somewhat pompously, 'is every-one's birthright.' He wanted to make the point that anyone could overcome their past, even if their history was as sordid as Nick's, but he needed an illustration. He scanned his brain for all the things which had upset him in childhood, but dying pets and being caught stealing *The Beano* in the village shop didn't seem quite traumatic enough to serve his purpose. Then, in a darkened, guilt-cluttered recess of his mind, he stumbled across his secret. 'We had a baby brother,' he began. 'Colm.'

Nick was listening. They were still in bed; still knotted on each other. The story came out lucid and distilled, as though the half-dreams and half-memories that formed it had coalesced in the years since it had been laid down.

'He was only a few weeks old. Tiny. I think I must have been about three, and Susan was no more than five. It was in the big sitting room at home, and Colm was in his pram. Susan and I had been left alone with him. We were playing at being weightlifters and Susan was teasing me for being so weedy. She could lift four volumes of the encyclopaedia above her head. I decided I'd show her how strong I was by lifting Colm out of his pram, which wasn't easy because the side of the pram was higher than my head and I had to stand on the wheels to do it. I'd just managed to pick him up when Susan saw what I was doing and came rushing over. She tried to take the baby from me. Between us we somehow managed to drop the baby on the floor. He lay very still and didn't cry. I've never known such fear in my life. Susan put him back in the pram and rearranged the blankets, and then he started howling. She told me not to tell anyone what had happened. My mother came in and we both played the innocent. We thought we'd got away with it. That night Colm died. There can't have been any bruises or anything because it was diagnosed as a cot death. Maybe it was, but Susan and I were convinced we'd killed him. She said that we'd go to prison if we were found out. Neither of us have ever mentioned it since, but it was always there, between us. Sometimes I wonder if I imagined the whole thing, because I dreamt of it so often and so vividly that it was hard to tell what really happened. But Mum kept photographs, of me and Susan either side of the pram, all smiling with pride at our baby brother. You're the first person I've ever told. I couldn't tell my mother, she was so hysterical about the death, like another person; she had always been so calm before. She and my father got very protective about us, which made the guilt worse, because I knew she would have hated me if she'd known what I did. Sometimes I wonder why Susan is so fussy about her own children, and then I remember. There's just a little glint of panic in her eyes if I pick one of them up. I spent my childhood thinking I was a murderer, and maybe that's why I tried to be so good, to make up for it.'

It wasn't until the end of the story that Aaron noticed the expression on Nick's face.

'Maybe,' Nick said, 'you shouldn't have told me that.'

'Why?'

'I thought you were good. I thought you were blameless. I thought you were someone I could trust.'

'What are you saying? I told you so that you'd know I wasn't so different from you.'

'I never killed a child.' Nick's voice was hard, and he was getting out of bed, reaching for clothes in a hurried way, as though a child murderer had no right to see him naked.

'I was a child myself. It was an accident. It was twenty-nine years ago. Surely if I can come to terms with it, you can.'

'Don't look for sympathy. You'll only make me sicker. There are some things you have no right to come to terms with.'

'Where are you going?'

'Anywhere. I don't want to be with you. I don't even want to look at you at the moment.'

'You said we had to be completely honest.'

Nick was walking out of the bedroom. 'To be completely honest,' he said, 'you disgust me.'

Then he was gone. Aaron heard the front door slam. For a long time he lay in bed, not moving. He couldn't understand what had gone wrong. He didn't know that Nick's relationship with him was based on the idea that they were not the same kind of person; that Aaron represented to Nick everything he wanted to and couldn't be. By divesting himself of his panoply for a moment Aaron had realised Nick's fear of disappointment.

'Fucking Mr fucking perfect,' were the words that Nick mostly repeated to himself as he walked towards the Twisted Arms. 'Fucking Mr fucking babykiller perfect. I knew it. I knew it. They're all the same.' He'd been waiting for a revelation like this. He knew, from deep and acrid experience, that no one could be as good as Aaron had pretended to be. He didn't know what was going to happen next, and didn't care much for the moment. The most urgent priority was that he needed a drink.

The chill-out crowd were in, making the most of the remains of the weekend. They all wanted to talk about Aaron, a lot of them having met him for the first time the night before. Nick found himself making the best of things; telling everyone how happy he and Aaron were together; how brilliant Aaron was and all the new schemes he kept coming up with; how famous people were always phoning (not, though, anyone that he had heard of before he'd met Aaron); how both Susan and Simon were barristers and had a real nanny to look after the children; how Aaron was going to fund the nightclub he was planning. By rubbing his friends' faces in his newly found good fortune, Nick gradually began to think that he had been too hasty in condemning Aaron. 'After all,' he told himself as he staggered back to the house at closing time, 'if he's no better than anyone else, I might as well stay with him as anyone. But there'll be no more Mr fucking perfect.'

Aaron was watching television. He had had an evening of paralysis and incomprehension, finally turning to the screen in the corner as though that might provide an explanation. It was, after all, one of the pivots on which Nick's mind seemed to turn. Flicking from channel to channel, he saw nothing but extremes. Audiences laughed heartily at feeble jokes. Those involved in drama were profoundly depressed or disturbed or angry. Every situation was a crisis. Even the News gave the impression that the world was about to end and that someone, usually someone unavailable for interview, was responsible. The more Aaron thought about it, the nearer he came to the conclusion that he was missing some vital piece of information by which Nick could be understood. The characters in the box had more in common with Nick than any real people he had ever encountered.

'Caught you,' Nick said from the hallway. 'Mr too high and mighty to have a telly in the house.'

'You're back.' Aaron spoke his welcome in a flat tone. At moments he had wondered if Nick was gone forever, and had been tormented by the sense of relief he had felt.

'This is my home too, isn't it?' Nick was grinning from ear to ear, obviously drunk and patently happier for it. 'You won't get rid of me that easily.'

'I wouldn't want to,' Aaron said. 'When I'm only beginning to understand what life is about.'

The most notable thing about the next few days was that Aaron found himself being fucked on several occasions. He wasn't sure what to think about that, but it seemed likely that there had been some kind of shift in the balance of power. Nick no longer bothered to pretend that there should be any kind of reciprocation. All attempts by Aaron to discuss it, or the events of Sunday for that matter, were met with a flint-hard response.

'Just don't push me. I'm having a hard enough time coming to terms with things as it is. I don't need this.'

There was little Aaron could do but make an outward show of accepting the blame, though, for what, he couldn't say.

In any case they both became busy. Aaron threw himself into the chicken breast project, calling his agent and publishers, and spending long hours in the kitchen and on the computer. Word got round that he was back and the phone would ring every ten minutes. Nick kept busy by going to the Twisted Arms for a bit of peace and quiet. For once in his life he was never short of the price of a drink, so there was always someone for him to talk to. Sometimes Aaron would drop in on his way back from a meeting, and it began to seem that people, with the exception of Cathy, were accepting him. He had started to watch the soaps and could now hold a normal conversation with almost anyone. A sort of pragmatic *status quo* descended on them. There wasn't time to rake over the past or worry about the future.

On Friday Aaron asked Nick if he would mind doing some shopping. Brian Yeats was coming to lunch the next day, but Aaron was too busy to go to the supermarket himself. He had arranged a meeting with his editor at the house in the afternoon to discuss the chicken book in detail. He gave Nick a list and the cashcard.

Nick left the house in an elated mood. The weather was clear and dry, the sky a tone brighter than the day before: one of those days when you realise that winter won't last forever. He loved the feeling of power that came with having a piece of plastic he could shove into a wall; and the proof that he was trusted to carry it. At Nick's prompting, Aaron had begun to talk about writing a will and putting the house in their joint names. Aaron thought it was the least he could do to prove his commitment.

With a self-discipline that he congratulated himself on, Nick confined his withdrawal to eighty pounds: enough to cover the shopping and a taxi home, and maybe a quick one in the pub. It was, he thought, so much more civilised than the usual awkward moment when Aaron would hand him cash. There was a dignity in using the card, as though the money were his own.

He was feeling far too cheerful to go straight to the dreary old supermarket and push a trolley round like some housewife, so he thought he'd have a pint first, to celebrate. At about five he phoned home and left a message on the answering machine to let Aaron know where he was. Nick had learned that Aaron appreciated such gestures. Aaron arrived at the Twisted Arms at six.

Nick was overjoyed to see him. When they were apart for a few hours, Nick would become mawkish about Aaron, longing for him in a way that was, somehow, never quite matched by the reality. Except that if Aaron appeared in the pub in one of his more beautiful suits, Nick would enjoy a thrill of pride, thinking, 'That's my boyfriend and everybody knows it.'

On this occasion Aaron was suitably dressed. He sat between Danielle and Nick and peered beneath the table. 'Hello,' he said, 'where's the shopping?'

'I haven't got it yet. Oh relax, for fuck's sake, and have a drink.'

Aaron looked at his watch. 'I'll go and get it now,' he said. 'With any luck it'll be late opening.'

'What's the rush?'

For an answer, Aaron merely flicked his eyes in Nick's direction. 'Did you get the money out?' he asked, with the same impatience.

'Only a bit.' Nick fished the cashcard out of his pocket and handed it over. 'You'll have to get more.'

Aaron was back in less than an hour, laden with carrier bags. He was able to relax then, have a drink and start talking to people.

'Fergus was in,' Nick said. 'That's what delayed me earlier. I hadn't seen him for so long we had a lot to catch up on.'

'Was Andrew with him?' Aaron asked the question in an automatic way, as though he had other things on his mind.

'No. They're finished long ago. Fergus has a new one now. Some sort of dancer or something.'

'A zookeeper,' Danielle corrected him.

'Zookeeper, dancer, whatever. Anyway he's having a party all day tomorrow. I said we'd go. He's looking forward to seeing you again.'

'You said what?' Aaron sounded incredulous.

'I know I should have asked you first, but it's Saturday tomorrow. You can't be working or anything.'

'Have you forgotten?'

'Forgotten what?'

'Brian Yeats is coming tomorrow. That's what the fucking shopping is supposed to be for.'

'Cancel him.'

'No, I fucking can't.'

'Well then you'll have to deal with him on your own. He's your friend. Nothing to do with me.'

'He's coming to meet you.'

'Now now,' Ed interrupted. 'Shouldn't you two be doing this at home like any normal couple?'

'I suppose,' Aaron said. 'We can go to Fergus' party after lunch.' His anger had been punctured by Ed's facetiousness.

'You see?' Nick said, crowing at his victory. 'Lot of fuss about nothing.'

Aaron hadn't brought the car, so they took a taxi home at closing time, because of all the shopping. The atmosphere was strained, and not helped by Aaron's sarcasm. 'Oh dear, what a waste of a day. Haven't you missed *Brookside*?'

Nick didn't rise to it, being half asleep for one thing and knowing that he could catch the omnibus edition the next day for another. His head cleared a little in the cold air between the taxi and the house. 'I need a drink,' he said. 'Shall we have a nightcap?'

Aaron sounded calm. 'I think you've probably had enough.' Nick decided to treat the remark as a joke.

'Not yet I haven't, sweetheart.'

They were in the sitting room by then, taking their coats off. 'I think,' Aaron said, 'eighty quids' worth in one afternoon should be enough for anyone.'

Nick was indignant. 'Been checking up on me, have you? Been saving that little gem until we got home? Or did you decide you'd embarrassed me enough in front of my friends for one evening?' He made towards the drinks cupboard, if only to show Aaron that he was the only one with the right to control his intake. Besides, with the way Aaron was behaving, Nick really did need a drink.

'I think you'll find that's empty,' Aaron said.

Nick opened the doors and discovered there wasn't a single bottle left. 'Where is it?'

'You've already drunk it. Or, I assume you have. I offered my editor a drink this afternoon, but when I went to look, all the bottles were empty. It was a bit embarrassing.'

'You could have gone to the offy.'

'That's not the point.'

Nick began to shout. 'What was the fucking stuff for if it wasn't to be fucking drunk?' While he was shouting he also did some fast thinking. 'There must be wine. You must have bought wine for the lunch tomorrow.' He made for the kitchen and the shopping bags.

'You won't find anything there,' Aaron called after him. 'I thought it was time we went on the wagon for a bit.'

It sounded to Nick as if Aaron were taunting him. He felt he was being trapped, and that his head would explode if he didn't get a drink. He started kicking things, looking in the bin for the empty bottles from the cupboard. There was always a dreg somewhere if you wanted it badly enough. There was a maddening tutting noise behind him, and Aaron was leaning against the doorpost, looking at him as though he was something unpleasant.

'Now you don't think,' Aaron said, 'I'd be as ecologically unsound as all that, do you? They're in the bottle bank at the bottom of the road. I think it's time we had a talk about this, but perhaps after you've been asleep for a few hours.'

Nick was not going to be spoken to like that. The rage had taken hold of him before he had a chance to see it coming. All the hate he had ever felt could now be directed at Aaron. His eyes became black with panophobia. He saw Aaron change into something hideous and threatening. The voice that Nick used when he spoke was as deep as the source of evil. 'What makes you think I'd talk to someone like you? Child-murdering scum. The sight of you makes me want to vomit.' Hearing the clarity of his own words made Nick feel powerful. Fear and anger, separately, were emotions he could control most of the time, but together they could take him over.

At that stage a vestigial shred of sanity still clung to his brain. He knew that if he didn't get away from Aaron things would take a turn for the worse. This had happened too often before, with too many other people. If he could just get to the bedroom, he knew that he was drunk enough to be unconscious in minutes, and the monster might be gone by the morning, if Aaron left him alone in the meantime.

Aaron was not to know any of this. He saw the change in Nick, like something in a cheap horror film, and all he could think was that he had caused the change, and it was his duty to effect the reversal. As Nick tried to pass him in the doorway, he reached out to touch his arm. 'Look. It's only me. Calm down.'

Nick squealed like a pig being slaughtered, and struck out. The next half an hour was a blur of flailing limbs and crashing furniture and screams from Nick that he was being murdered and someone should call the police. Aaron, being stronger and less drunk, would pin him to the floor and plead with him to stop, but every time he let go, Nick would lunge at him again. Eventually, Nick feigned unconsciousness and Aaron left the room, desperate to think for a moment. While he was out, Nick phoned the police, who had already had a call from one of the neighbours and were on their way.

Aaron was still in a stupor of bewilderment when he answered the door to the two policemen. The only previous contact he had had with the forces of law was to ask directions in the street. When the uniformed men entered the house Nick magically resurrected himself and began yelling, 'Arrest him. He tried to kill me. Please. Take him away from me.'

It took all of Aaron's presence of mind to explain the situation, given that he didn't understand it himself. The officers, seeing how drunk Nick was and having established that Aaron was the householder, offered to remove Nick from the premises, but Aaron said, 'No. He has nowhere to go.' By this time Nick had worn himself out and was genuinely unconscious on the sofa. Aaron agreed that they should not both remain in the house, and said that he could go and stay with his sister.

When Nick woke a while later, both the police and Aaron were gone. He found a can of beer in the fridge and took it to bed with him. Though he only stayed awake long enough to drink half of it, he was calmer as a result, and slept until late the next morning.

Aaron did not stay at Susan's. He couldn't think what he might say to explain himself. He walked the streets for a couple of hours, trying to fathom what had happened, and had to admit that he had no answers. By the time he got home again he was so tired that he could barely fit the key in the lock of his front door. He checked on Nick in the bedroom and then made a bed for himself on the biggest sofa. 'At least,' he thought, as his mind darkened for sleep, 'he's going to have to talk about it now.'

Once again Nick woke to find Aaron, shaven, clean and dressed, sitting on the edge of the bed, looking at him. Nick was terrified, but he wasn't going to show it.

'Just keep away from me, you fucking monster. Don't you dare lay a finger on me.'

'Nick,' Aaron said. 'It's me, not a monster. I'm not going to hurt you.'

'You said that before. What about last night, then? Mr couldn't fucking hurt a fly perfect?' Nick's arms felt as though they had been wrenched out of their sockets, so he had some grounds for suspecting that the violence had not been one-sided. He also had a bruise below his left eye, but he wasn't aware of that yet.

'We've got to talk,' Aaron said. 'And we don't have much time. Brian's going to be here in a few hours.'

Nick began to be aware that he was no longer in any physical danger. Aaron was being so rational that he was infected by the calm. As he became fully awake and his mind began to clear, the night before took on an unreal aspect. Talking about it was the last thing he wanted to do. Besides, his bladder was at bursting point.

His first thoughts as he straddled the lavatory, were that he had blown it. He wondered if Paul was likely to take him in, and whether Aaron would leave him alone in the house to pack. There were a few nice things around which Aaron probably wouldn't miss, and far more clothes in the wardrobes than one person could possibly need. Thinking about all the things he couldn't take with him made him speculate whether the situation wasn't beyond salvation. After all, Aaron had said that he wanted to talk. Nick wiped himself with difficulty. He ached all over, but that was not an unfamiliar feeling for him on the morning after a heavy night. Not being in the habit of looking in the mirror first thing, he still didn't know about the bruise. He decided to see how the land lay. He looked in at the sitting room and the kitchen. They were in a bit of a state, but nothing that couldn't be remedied. It was just a question of persuading Aaron that last night had been no more than a routine domestic spat that got out of control.

'We have to talk.' Aaron was standing behind him.

Suddenly, Nick became very efficient. 'Look, there isn't time for that now. Help me get this cleared up before your friend sees it. You make a start while I get dressed.'

'It's more important to talk. I need to understand this. It's completely outside my experience. I don't want it to happen again, ever.'

'It's not going to happen again. Come on, get a move on.'

Nick went and shut himself in the bathroom again while Aaron tidied. That was when he finally noticed the bruising. It was not noticeably sore yet, but it was colourful enough to get the sympathy he would need. There weren't any marks on Aaron's face, so apportioning blame for the fight in Nick's favour was going to be easy. Nick realised that he could turn the whole disaster to his advantage.

The house had been set to rights by the time Nick was ready. There were smells of cooking coming from the kitchen.

'Can we talk now?' Aaron asked, sounding firmer than Nick considered he had any right to be.

Nick pointed at the bruise. 'What about this then?'

'I know. That's what frightens me.'

'Not as much as it frightens me. You terrified me last night. I thought I trusted you.'

Aaron was foxed. 'What are you saying?'

'Never struck anyone in your life? It takes experience to do this sort of damage.'

'Are you saying that I did that to you?'

'Who else could it have been? I've got witnesses. The police saw what was going on. I only have to go to a doctor and you're on a charge, matey.'

'You did that yourself. You fell against the side of the table.'

'That old chestnut.' Nick had to admit that Aaron was playing according to the script. The side of the table was one he'd often used himself in the same situation. 'Please,' he said. 'You're only making it worse for yourself. At least I can be honest about these things. You can drop the perfect act. I know about you, remember?'

'I didn't hit you. The most I did last night was hold you down to stop you damaging both of us. We have to talk about this properly, or it's going to happen again.'

Nick decided it was time to broaden the subject. 'Have you decided how you're going to explain it to your Brian friend?'

'No. That isn't the point.'

'Of course it's the point. What if your sister gets to hear of it? She's the one person, apart from me, who knows what you're capable of. We're going to say that I was mugged last night. Most people are too intelligent to believe the falling over story.'

Aaron was almost sick with frustration. He wasn't that clear what had happened in the flurry of violence. He only knew that he could not have done anything deliberate to hurt Nick. The bruise frightened him, and he wasn't accustumed to fear. 'Tell people what you like,' he capitulated. 'But we still have to sort things out. It's possible to get help for a problem like yours. I thought I could deal with it on my own, but I can't.'

'My problem? Why does it have to be my problem? You're the one with a track record. I haven't killed anyone yet.'

'Can we drop the child-murderer thing? I was talking about your drinking.'

'Dropping things,' Nick said, 'is your speciality. I can smell something burning in the kitchen.'

'They're aubergines,' Aaron said. 'They're supposed to burn.' He went to check on them anyway.

Lunch wasn't nearly such a trial as Nick had feared it would be. Brian brought a bottle of wine. When he produced it, Aaron told him that he and Nick were giving up drink for Lent. 'Speak for yourself sweetie,' Nick said, taking the bottle out of Brian's hands. Brian was affable enough for the conversation to be general and pleasant, mostly about India. Things were almost spoilt by one caustic remark of Aaron's. He said to Nick, 'Anyone would think you'd been to some of those places from the way you talk.'

Brian was pleased, taking this as an indication that the shine was going off the relationship already. He couldn't say that he liked Nick, but neither could he say that Nick was as bad as Susan had made out. That afternoon Brian decided that the best policy would be to steer clear of Aaron until the dust had settled. Meanwhile, Nick was enjoying giving them details about the mugging, and modestly played down his heroism in tackling three thugs single-handed.

Aaron was a bad host that day. Remaining silent while Nick lied to Brian on their behalf was painful to him in a way that was almost physical. He couldn't eat and he thought his head would burst. For him, a friendship depended on truth and his definition of a friend was someone with whom he could be completely honest. There were some who had been offended by him and drifted away over the years, but those who remained were people he felt he could count on. Brian was chief among these, and the single person whose approval of Nick would have counted. The object of this lunch had been for Brian and Nick to get to like each other. Now, Aaron was watching it happen on a false premise. 'And did I,' he asked himself, 'fall in love with him on a false premise?' The thought seared through his head as though a nerve had been exposed in one of his molars. It was not, he told himself, the time to be thinking like that. He was impatient for Brian to be gone so that the lies could be cleared from the air, and his impatience showed. Brian declined the offer of coffee.

The hiatus of lunch had given him one or two new ways to phrase his conviction that Nick and he needed to talk. Brian was hardly out of the door and the dishes were still congealing on the table when he declared, 'We have to deal with this. If we can't do it between us, there is always professional help. I am not going through another night like last night. I was effectively thrown out of my own house by the police, did you know that?'

Nick was making himself comfortable on the sofa, Hu settling on his chest as though they were going to have a nap together. 'Maybe,' he said, 'that will make you stop and think the next time you feel like dishing out black eyes.'

'For shit's sake,' Aaron began.

'It's no use denying it. I'm the one with the bruise. Now, if you don't mind, I'm tired. I've just spent an hour and a half helping you convince your doctor friend that you're not the monster you really are.'

'Nick,' Aaron said, in a sort of pleading voice he had never heard himself use before, 'I don't understand. You're the only one who can help me to understand what's going on here. I feel as though I'm losing my mind.'

'At last.' Nick smiled. 'You finally admit you're not superman. What does it feel like to be human then? Like the rest of us?'

'Frightening,' Aaron admitted.

'Good. Now you know how I feel all the time. You just have to live with it, and remember you can always get pissed when things get a bit too much.'

'How did this happen?' Aaron was under the delusion that the dialogue was constructive in some way.

'Two men who hardly know each other really, living on top of one another, twenty-four hours a day. Things are bound to get out of hand from time to time.'

'What should we do about it? Do you think you should move out for a while?'

'Oh you're trying to kick me out now are you? At the first sign of trouble. I thought this was supposed to be *our* home. Two days ago you were about to put it in joint names.'

'I'm not kicking you out. You know that.'

'So I get to live in some crummy bedsit while you go on lording it up here. How's that going to make me feel about myself? I feel inadequate enough already.'

'Look, forget I said it. I'm only trying to make things good again. We have to do something.'

'Do we indeed?'

'Have you thought about Alcoholics Anonymous?'

'That's right. Look for a scapegoat. Anything that'll let you off the hook. So I'm an alcoholic now, am I? Well let me tell you, I've been conned into that one before. Do you remember that bloke called John, in Priapus?'

'The one who wanted the money?'

'Him. That fight last night was nothing compared to the fights we used to have. He was a real psycho. He got me feeling so bad about myself that he persuaded me to go to those meetings. It didn't make anything better. If I learned one thing from that AA crowd, it was that I wasn't an alcoholic at all. I can take a drink as well as the next man. It turned out that John was the alcoholic all along. I'm not falling for that one again.'

Aaron could think of no response, so he went to clear the table and wash up instead, wondering how it was that life had become so complicated. He counted through the events again and again. Sometimes it appeared that none of it was his fault and sometimes he thought of things he could have done differently. If he had trusted Nick more in the first place, he wouldn't have come racing back from Mysore and none of this would have happened. They would have got used to the idea of each other and Nick would have had time to establish his business. Aaron blamed himself for not having stuck to the original plan. He shouldn't have told Nick about Colm's death, at least not until they were ready to deal with such things. Having spoken about it had stirred up all the childhood nightmares in Aaron, and the long-tarnished needles of guilt were polished and sharp again, which didn't help him to remain calm in his present situation.

He was, however, beginning to see things from Nick's perspective. Before, whenever he had thought about the future, it had seemed to him a succession of endless possibilities. That is how he had seen possibilities in Nick. Now the future had taken on the colour of Nick's point of view, and there was only a terrifying blank expanse of time that had to be filled somehow. A life of drink and soaps was tempting, each filling the gaps between the other, until every day could be dealt with without thinking. He would not be the first one to have striven for happiness and settled for oblivion.

That, he told himself, hunched over the washing-up from an ache of tension across the back of his neck (these days the muscles of his back and neck seemed to be made of concrete), wasn't good enough. He, Aaron, was the strong one, the one with something to give. If he couldn't take one human and love him into goodness, then the whole of his life and everything he had believed in was a sham. Aaron believed in goodness the way others believed in God or Capitalism. He wanted to be a good person in the way that others want wealth or fame or power. He voted socialist and gave pound coins to the homeless and fed stray cats. He could listen to someone else's problems for hours without showing any signs of boredom. He campaigned against unjust laws and did his shopping and investing with political correctness. By some fluke, he had always been rewarded for his troubles. If he turned down a job because he couldn't square it with his conscience, a better paid and guilt-free job would be offered to him the next day. His life had been like one of those comic strips where the cheerful and resourceful hero always finishes by being rewarded with a slap-up tea at the fish and chip shop with his chums. It was no accident then that he had fallen in love with someone like Nick, at a time when he was looking for a new direction. Like an evangelist, having secured his own faith he had set out to spread the word. Not that that was the reason he had fallen in love. That had more to do with an accident of physical attraction. It was, however, the reason he was stuck with that love; the reason he couldn't give up on Nick. The more it became obvious that Nick needed his help, the more they were tied together. As he dried his plates and put them away (his beautiful, kelp-green plates), he knew that unless he could save Nick he might lose his faith in himself. It might seem, at that moment, as though they were sliding towards Nick's level, but things, he told himself, often look their worst before they begin to get better.

Feeling more cheerful, he woke Nick from his nap, and they went to Fergus' party. It was a bit like being in Goa again, with a lot of the same people and a similar quantity of drugs in circulation. By the time they reached Priapus, at midnight, it was as though the wounds were beginning to heal. The Ecstasy was good, was gentle stuff, and they spent the night in one another's arms like lovers, telling each other that this was what being together was all about.

Sunday was just one of those mindless, tooth-grinding, bed-ridden, huggy come-downs, as though Friday night had never happened. They smoked an eighth of dope between them and fell in love again. Even Nick was so off his guard as to be capable of admission. 'What was that all about?' he asked, as though speaking of something they had witnessed from afar.

'You tell me,' Aaron mumbled, too comfortable to lift his head to speak.

'I get the devil in me sometimes. I don't know what happens, but I can't help it.'

'And what should I do,' Aaron asked, 'when it happens?'

'Get away,' Nick said, sounding even to himself as though he was speaking the truth. 'Get right away, as far away as possible, until it's over. I don't want us to hurt each other.'

LAUGHTER ∫

Without telling Nick, Aaron made an appointment with a counselling service for people who were involved with addicts. He found himself in a seedy room at the back of a mental hospital, describing Nick and their relationship to an unsmiling man with bad teeth, called Malcolm, if the plastic label on his cardigan was anything to go by. Malcolm listened attentively for twenty minutes, asking questions that were, to Aaron, astonishingly perceptive. Then he told Aaron to get out of the relationship as fast as possible.

'That's not what I came here for.'

'What did you come here for?'

'To find out what I can do.'

'Leave him.'

'No. To find out what I can do to help. You're a professional. You must deal with people like him all the time. You must know how I can begin to make things right.'

'There is nothing,' Malcolm said, 'you can do, but save yourself.'

'I'm all right. It's him I'm worried about. I think he might be suicidal.'

'Has he mentioned suicide?'

'No, but he's so afraid, of everything. He can't walk down the road unless he has a drink inside him. And he's so self-destructive. I think the only thing that's stopping him is that he's as terrified of death as he is of life.'

'How much do you know about projection?'

'As much as any layman. I can't see the relevance of it here. Are you saying that I'm the one who's suicidal?'

'You're the one who's talking about it. From what you described, he's not destroying himself. He's destroying you, and you're the one who's letting him.'

'I want to help him. I love him.'

'What do you love?'

'What do you mean?'

'Do you love him as he is, the addict, or do you love the person he could be? Addicts survive. They might achieve recovery, but they'll always be what they are. It's people like you who get destroyed.'

'You can't just write him off like that. He didn't set out to be what he is. He's angry.'

'Anger, in my experience, is a symptom of fear.'

'That's what I'm trying to tell you: he's afraid. He has been fucked around all his life, especially by those who claimed to love him.'

'So he's afraid of being loved? Yes? Admit it. You are supplying him with the thing he probably fears most, which is love. You've said as much. You could get him into therapy, and you might well have something to show for your trouble at the end of it, but he wouldn't be the man you want him to be. You'd lose him in any case. And even that is unlikely. I'd have to meet him for myself, but the person you described to me is someone who isn't ready. He sounds as though he has years of drinking left in him before he hits rock bottom, and when he does, the only one who can help him is himself. He'll resent you for not being able to do something which was outside your power in the first place. The more you love him, the worse things will get. And if he loves you, the more he will feel guilty and afraid, and angry. You've got yourself into something complicated, and you should get out while you can, for both your sakes.'

'What if it's too late for that?'

'I won't say it's never too late, but the fact that you've come here shows that you're still capable of saving yourself.'

'I'm all right. It's him I'm worried about.'

'Leaving him is the only thing you can do to help him.'

'I can't. I've made promises. I couldn't betray him. That's what everyone else has done. He needs someone he can trust. And I believe in him.'

Aaron spoke the last words quietly. A few seconds of silence followed, and Malcolm said, 'I shouldn't be saying this. I am, as you say, a professional, but I know what you are thinking: the way you are thinking. I've been in this situation. It was worse for me, because I am a professional. I thought I was the best person to deal with it, and I stayed for longer than I should. I know how these things end. I lost everything, including my own self-esteem, which is something you can never recover completely. I'm telling you: while you are with him, you have a problem as much as he has. You have to give him up, just as he has to stop drinking.'

'He isn't just an alcoholic, you know. He isn't just a disease.'

'I know. They never are.'

Aaron left with a feeling of light-headedness, of the kind you have when you are told of the death of someone close to you. He didn't want to believe what he had heard, or think about the things he had said. The advice had been based only on the account he had given. Had he given another account, the advice might have been different; might have been the advice he had wanted to hear. He couldn't rid himself of the thought that he had betrayed Nick.

He found him in the Twisted Arms, chatting and grinning

and being himself, and it was easy to discount everything that Malcolm had said. Aaron reasoned that his love was an exceptional thing, beyond the theories of professionals or the experience of others. He decided that he wasn't going to give in so easily. He would prove that he had been right all along.

The first ruse which occurred to Aaron in the campaign to reform his lover was a refreshing weekend in the country. Away from Priapus and the Twisted Arms and the normal binge of drugs and pick-me-ups, Aaron reasoned that the breaking of one habit would lead to the breaking of others. Not wanting Nick to feel threatened, he phrased his proposition with less teetotalitarian motives.

'You haven't met my parents yet.'

It was Wednesday morning. Aaron had been up and working since seven. Nick appeared at eleven-thirty, cheerful and relaxed and wearing a white cotton jumper of Aaron's, which Aaron never wore himself because it wasn't worth the labour of washing it every two seconds. The bruise on Nick's face was developing nicely in shades of blue and mahogany, making Aaron wince involuntarily every time he caught sight of it.

'Morning, sweet pea. That smells nice.' Nick lifted the lid from a saucepan and breathed in, the way husbands are inclined to do on advertisements for instant sauces. Earlier, when he had woken, he had had a worse than usual sense of dread at the thought of coming downstairs. Sometimes it wasn't so bad, because Aaron would be out, but today he could hear the low, sporadic sounds of spices being ground and the telephone being answered. So, he would have to think of an excuse to leave the house if he wanted to go to the pub; he would have that uncomfortable sensation that he was being disapproved of, in an unspoken way, when he turned the television on. Worse than anything, there was the constant threat that Aaron would want to talk: little verbal excavations that he couldn't deal with in the unavoidable sobriety of morning time. For a while, Nick had stayed beneath the duvet, with his face screwed up and his hands shaking until, in an ambush of pragmatism, he had decided to take two of the Goan valium and have a good long wank while his nerves settled. By the time he drifted into the kitchen he felt ready to deal with whatever the following twelve hours might throw at him.

'Don't do that,' Aaron said. 'You're letting the steam out. I was going to call home this afternoon, but I thought I'd ask you first. We don't have any plans for this weekend, do we?'

'I don't know.' Nick spoke cautiously. He had a presentiment of what was about to be proposed, and some of the goodwill brought on by the valium was being eroded by it. Dealing with Susan had been bad enough, and that was on home territory. From what he had heard, and seen in photographs, he was rattled at the thought of meeting the Gunn parents. They lived in a big house and walked around with dogs at their heels. The mother owned a riding school – and the father a trout farm. They had an Aga and always wore shit-green clothes. Aaron denied that they were gentry, but they could have passed for it, and often did, in the version that Nick recounted to his friends.

'I thought,' Aaron said, 'we could go down for the weekend. I haven't seen them for months.'

'I'm sure they'd rather see you on your own. There's no reason for me to go.'

'I thought you might like to get away from everything.'

'I haven't anything to wear.'

'It's the middle of nowhere.' Aaron found it easier to argue with Nick while he was cooking, the need to watch what he was doing obviating the possibility of eye contact. 'You don't need anything except a pair of wellingtons and a big jumper.'

'I've never, in my life, owned a pair of wellingtons. Or a big jumper.'

'Borrow some off me.'

'What, and have your parents see me in your cast-offs? No thanks.'

'We'll get you some of your own. That's settled then. I thought we could leave early on Saturday morning and avoid the traffic.'

Thinking about it afterwards, Nick blamed the valium for the ease with which he had been defeated. He had no intention of going anywhere near the country at the weekend, but thought it would be safer to present an excuse at the last moment, when it would be more difficult for Aaron to come up with counter-arguments. In the meantime, it was better not to think about it.

On Friday the heating broke down. Nick was woken by a chill in the air. He dressed without washing and went to find Aaron, who was in his office, wearing an overcoat and bashing away at his computer.

'I've called the plumber,' Aaron said. 'He's away. Can't come until Monday.'

'What are we going to do? We can't live like this.'

'It's only for one day. We won't be here tomorrow.'

For a moment Nick thought it might be a trick. Aaron might have turned the heating off to make the house uninhabitable so that there was no way out of going away. 'I'm freezing,' he said, in a bad tempered way. 'I can see my own breath. Look.'

'It's not that bad. You can always make up a fire in the sitting room grate if you're desperate.'

'Can't you get another plumber?'

'No. Stop making a fuss. I was brought up without central heating. You just put more clothes on.'

'Some of us are used to civilisation,' Nick said. 'I'm going to the pub. For a bit of heat.'

'Are you coming back for lunch?'

'Can I borrow a tenner?' Nick always mumbled when he asked that. It made him angry that he should have to ask at all. Fortunately, Aaron was so vague about money that, as often as not, Nick could just take some that was lying around without, apparently, the loss being noticed.

'My wallet's in the hall,' Aaron said. He was distracted by a debate he was having with himself; whether chicken breast with preserved lemon should include pistachios or not. He was trying to put together, from memory, something he had tasted in a Moroccan restaurant several years before.

It was a bitter day, with a dry wind from the north. Nick's mind was full of blame as he walked, with his chin in his chest and his fists in his pockets. He was being driven out of the house by the cold. That he would have chosen to spend his day in the pub anyway did not affect his reasoning. He should have been able to call for a taxi. He could afford it (he had, interpreting a tenner metaphorically, taken thirty pounds from the wallet), but he knew that Aaron, with the thrift of the rich, considered taxis an extravagance. In a while his pique was soothed by a fantasy he often engaged in, where he had control of the purse strings and Aaron had to come crawling to him for money. Which reminded him that Aaron had not yet made an appointment with the solicitor, as he had promised, so that they could draw up mutually beneficial wills. The thought of how well off he was going to be after Aaron's death comforted him further, until it was punctured by guilt. 'But I'd miss him so much,' he told himself, 'that I couldn't bear to be poor as well.' He allowed himself to grieve for Aaron's fictitious death for a few hundred yards and, by the time he reached the pub, he had got to the stage of widowhood where time would heal the wounds and he could bravely begin to enjoy life again. 'It's what he would have wanted,' he thought, as he pushed through the door and into the warmth.

Fergus had taken the day off work and was sitting at the table by the pinball machine with two or three newspapers in front of him. Nick sat down and they began to talk about Aaron. Rather, Fergus asked how Aaron was and Nick began to talk about him.

'I love that man. I love him as much as it's possible for one human to love another. I even love the way he always tries to pretend he's perfect.'

'Maybe he is.'

'No one is. He just can't admit it. If you knew him like I do. I keep telling him we should just try to be ordinary, but he has this artistic temperament. I have problems, I admit. I'm not proud of it, but everyone has skeletons in their closet. Most people muddle through, have a few drinks and the odd affair, but not Aaron. At least, that's what he pretends most of the time. Then it all comes out in a big gush, and the next day he's back to Mr perfect again. He needs me if he's going to sort himself out. Did you know he killed his own brother?'

'Aaron?'

'It was a long time ago. Don't tell him I told you.'

'By accident?'

'Sort of. Anyway, he got away with it. But that sort of thing isn't easy to live with, especially if you won't face up to it.'

'How did it happen?'

'I suppose he lost control. I just thought you should know, in case anything happens to me.' Here, Nick put the tips of his fingers to his black eye and winced.

'Did he do that?'

Nick shrugged.

'I thought you said you were mugged.'

'We had to say something. I didn't want my friends to think he was violent. You know how protective people can be. It was just a spat, really. I've dealt out enough bruises in my time to know the score. It won't happen again. There's always a few little hiccups at the start of a relationship.'

'Are you sure?'

Nick was prevented from answering by the arrival of Ed. Thereafter the conversation ran along more general lines. By mid-afternoon the pub was beginning to fill with the weekend crowd. There were several parties being talked about. Nick, thinking he had enough ammunition to evade spending the weekend away, and becoming sentimental at the thought of two days apart from the man he loved, phoned Aaron and begged him to come over. Aaron, whose fingers had turned so blue that he was mishitting the keys on the computer, agreed.

Aaron arrived as Fergus was in the middle of recounting his experiences of the night before, with a couple he'd pulled at an underwear party on the other side of the river. The sex, he said, had been great, but he was woken in the middle of the night by the two boys having a row. Fergus was pinned beneath them while they screamed and hit each other. One of them was bleeding from the nose and Fergus was splattered all over with blood. He said that was why he hadn't been able to face going into work that morning.

Nick was laughing, even though Fergus couldn't see the humour in it himself. 'Oh come on,' Nick said. 'You have to admit. It's a good story.' As the evening wore on, and Nick drank more (he had just run out of money when he phoned Aaron, but now he was in funds again), he kept thinking of jokes at Fergus' expense, and constantly brought the conversation back to the subject of the tricky threesome, as he called it.

Aaron, watching Nick laugh, black-eyed, thought the whole thing was uncomfortably close to the bone. He began to wonder if he was doing the right thing in taking Nick home for the weekend, but it was too late to back out. Things, he told himself, would be different in the morning. He was too preoccupied to notice the strange looks which Fergus was giving him.

Nick was still in high spirits when they reached home. Since he hadn't eaten that day, he flopped down on the sofa and commanded Aaron to make him a bacon sandwich.

'If you really want one, you can make it yourself for a change,' Aaron said. 'I'm going to bed. We have to be up at six.'

'You have to be up at six.' Nick hadn't yet announced his intention of staying, but now seemed as good a time as any. Aaron, taking his contradiction for drunken forgetfulness, foiled him by going upstairs without responding.

In a fit of defiance, Nick made the sandwich and ate it in front of the telly. The house was so cold that he would have preferred to eat in bed, but he was so angry with Aaron that he thought he might choke if he tried. He was halfway through a mouthful when Aaron reappeared, naked, and said something that he couldn't quite catch.

'What?' Nick said, spitting out a shower of crumbs and bits of rind. Aaron would have to speak up if he wanted to be heard over the telly.

Aaron crossed the room and turned down the volume on the set. Nick was amazed that a body which could turn him on so much when he was in the mood could be so disgusting at other times. He thought that Aaron could, at least, have put a dressing gown on to cover his goose-bumped flesh.

'I was listening to that,' Nick said.

'And so was the rest of the street. I couldn't sleep with it. If you have to watch television all night, at least you could try to keep it down.'

Nick reached for the remote and put the sound up as high as it would go. Aaron turned the set off. Nick heaved himself off the sofa and switched it on again, like Hardy to a nude and taller Laurel. Aaron yanked the plug out and left the room.

Nick was beyond thinking. No one was going to push him around like that. He couldn't remember what he had been watching, but it was the principle that counted. He was sick of being dictated to in what was supposed to be his own home. He replugged the television and pretended to settle down to his sandwich again, knowing that Aaron would return. This time Nick would be ready for him. There was an Indian wooden horse, about thirteen inches high, on the table behind the sofa. Nick weighed it in his hand and put it beneath the cushion beside him.

Aaron, still naked, was doing his best to stay calm.

'Have you gone out of your mind?' Aaron had to shout to be heard above the television.

'If I'm mad, you've driven me to it. I hate you. You're evil and I hate you.' Nick had to shout to make his feelings on the matter understood.

Aaron went to a drawer on the other side of the room, opened it, and took out a large pair of scissors. Nick, thinking he was about to be stabbed, shouted, 'Don't think you'll get away with this. All my friends know about you.' At the same time he gripped the wooden horse.

Aaron ignored him, and bent down by the television, pulled the plug out again and cut through the cord. That, for Nick, was the last straw. He charged from behind.

Somehow, reeling from the blow to the back of his head, Aaron succeeded in shaking Nick off his back and ran upstairs. Nick was still dialling the police when he came down again, fully dressed. He had never thought it possible to dress so quickly. Without pausing, he made straight for the front door. Nick dropped the receiver and ran after him into the street, stocking-footed and brandishing the horse.

Aaron managed to get into his car and away, with Nick hanging onto the door handle with one hand and beating on the roof of the car with the horse in the other. By the end of the street he had to let go, and Aaron was gone.

Aaron, his mind a blank, drove in the direction of the countryside. For two and three-quarter hours he thought about nothing but the road in front of him. He had got away; he had done the right thing. Tomorrow he could begin to think. He didn't know what he was going to think, but he knew that he would think something. Tomorrow he would wake up in his old bed and hear the squirrels thumping in the attic above him and he would know what to do. He always knew what to do, except now. After two and three-quarter hours he passed the first signpost for his parents' village, and shortly afterwards drove over a patch of black ice on a steep bend going downhill. In normal circumstances he might have been able to control the car, but there was something wrong with his head, and he couldn't think. As the car spun and rolled, he thought, 'I'm going to die. Thank God it's all over.'

It was like sobriety, but it could not have been. It was rage turned to coldness and fear turned to destruction. Nick stood on the pavement for a second or two, until the frost penetrated his socks and began to burn the soles of his feet. Aaron had left him, and he hated him for it. The only thing that mattered now was that Aaron should suffer; should be made to understand how Nick had suffered. Back inside the house he picked up the telephone and dialled the number he had been dialling a minute before.

'I want to report a stolen car.' He gave the number of the yellow Capri, and said that his name was Aaron Gunn. With any luck Aaron would spend the night in a cell. That would do for a start. Even if Aaron managed to wriggle out of the stolen car thing, he would be breathalysed. Let him see what life was like without a driving licence.

As he smashed the receiver into its cradle, Nick saw the severed flex of his television. Two could play at the wilful destruction of property. He began to look for the right kind of instrument. A golf club would have been ideal, a sledgehammer even better. As he searched his anger mounted, cursing Aaron for having nothing to hand which could be used as a weapon. What, he asked himself, if they were burgled? How were they expected to protect themselves?

Eventually he found a claw hammer, in a tool kit under the stairs. It was not unlike a hammer he had used once before, a long time before; but that had not been his fault; there had been provocation, just as there was provocation now; and he had not been caught, or suspected, which was the main thing; and he had suffered for it, in his own mind, suffered enough to make him angry, dreaming sometimes of a skull that gave way beneath the head of a claw hammer. That was his secret, the one that Aaron, for all his bleeding heart sympathy, couldn't winkle out of him. Aaron should count himself lucky that the hammer had not been to hand earlier.

Can there be such a thing as a methodical frenzy? He smashed wildly, but smashed the things that would hurt Aaron most. He smashed the oven; the stainless steel beloved oven. He made bits of the computer; the fragile, fact-filled machine from which Aaron made his living. The deep green plates, the heavy tumblers, the paper-thin eighteenth century wine glasses, the radio tuned to Radio 4, the coffee grinder (he can fucking well drink instant, like anyone else). He would have liked to smash the big mirror over the fireplace, which Aaron said had belonged to his grandmother, but that would have brought seven years' bad luck, and that was a risk Nick wasn't prepared to take. It was not blind anger; it was something else. Only he could have understood what he was doing, and he was the least likely person to analyse it.

When he was tired of smashing, and had noticed that his fingers were bleeding from the flying glass, he set to ripping, which was even more methodical; therapeutic, almost. One snip from the scissors, and a long tear: every suit and jacket became a mound of strips on the bedroom floor. There was something calming in that exercise. Before he had quite finished, he had begun to cry; the weeping of a tantrum in subsidence. The destruction slowed, and the heat of his exertion dissipated. Soon he was not much more than afraid, which was normal, though he was more afraid than normal, and cold, which he could do something about.

If you're desperate, Aaron had said, you can make a fire up in the sitting room grate. Desperate seemed a fair description. What was there to burn? The wooden horse was lying where he had dropped it. He made a bed of pages torn from a book (a 1911 edition of Don Quixote, with 700 illustrations: some blinking heirloom or other, something Aaron treated with reverence, that was only asking to be burned), and set the horse on top. There was burning, after a fashion, but the tears that started warm on his cheekbones were still icy on his chin. There was no longer any satisfaction in this. The next thing to be dealt with was his own exhaustion, and Nick went to bed, not without thinking that he could do with a drink.

Hu, who had been hiding beneath the sofa during all the noise, came out after a time, and picked his way with feline delicacy between the shards and splinters. Finding a warm body already in the bed, he settled down to sleep, without washing, coiled in the wedge between Nick's thighs and ankles.

The weather, next morning, was inappropriately cheerful. Clean, ozone-free, spring sunshine came through the windows (the curtains lay, ribboned, on the floor) and shone on Nick's closed eyes, like an interrogating light. His first moments were always clear of memory. There was the ritual of establishment: who he was and who the presence was in bed beside him. The cat stretched, and yawned. The house was silent, and cold. Something was not right, and he couldn't remember what it was, and he knew that he didn't want to remember either. There was a struggle between remaining where he was, in ignorance, and the need to empty his bladder. He considered pissing himself, but he had tried that one before, and regretted it. He could make it to the bathroom with eyes half closed. There was no need to know, just yet.

The hands that held his cock were streaked with dried blood. Could the worst have happened? Was Aaron lying somewhere in the house with his head smashed in? He had got away with that once, it would be too much to hope that he could get away with it a second time. These circumstances were altogether different. That had been in a city where no one knew him; where no one had seen him come or go. There had been months of terror that he might be discovered, but he was not. That had been a secret affair;

a love that had gone on undeclared outside a few rooms in strange cities. If, he thought, he had killed Aaron, then he had finally gone too far.

There was no sign of a body in the flat and, in looking through the debris, pieces of the night before came back to him. Aaron was gone. He could remember standing on the pavement in the cold. He could remember hanging on to the door handle as the car drove away. That bastard, he thought, could have killed me doing that.

Hu gavotted round his ankles, making a request for breakfast. 'I don't know about you,' Nick said, 'but I'm not hanging round this fucking kip.' The house was trashed. Nick went through the options. First, to phone the police and report a burglary. That was quickly dismissed. He had a record for this kind of thing. In the unlikely event the police believed him, Aaron himself probably wouldn't. He had to face it. His time with Aaron was probably finished. There was no going back from this one. 'Why,' he asked Hu, 'are all men the same, in the end? Why can't I find someone who'll just let me be myself?'

Second option: to clear out. If Aaron tried to press charges, he could say that they'd had a row and Aaron had done most of the damage. He still had the bruise to show that Aaron was violent. His word against Aaron's. He knew how to be plausible in the law courts, and he could always threaten to tell the tabloids that Aaron was a baby-killer.

Becoming aware of the dreadful need for a cigarette, he never got past the second option. A cigarette, and a drink, ideally. His packet, lying undisturbed among the chaos of the sitting room, was empty. He searched for money, and found almost nineteen pounds in change, in a box on Aaron's dressing table. 'Bingo,' he said.

The man at the corner shop sold him a bottle of whisky, twenty cigarettes, and three scratchcards. Normally, he only bought one scratchcard at a time, but today he felt in need of cheering up. The first card won him a ten pound prize.

'There you are,' the man behind the counter said. 'It must be your lucky day.'

Believing that it might be, he bought ten more scratchcards with his prize money.

'Lucky, lucky, lucky,' the man said.

'I should bloody well hope so. I'm due a bit of luck, after all I've been through.'

The man didn't appear to show any interest in the details of Nick's misfortunes, but Nick told him anyway. 'I've been beaten up, dumped, had the car stolen.'

'The times we live in,' the man said.

Nick was scratching away at his twelve cards. The first win, he reasoned, had to be a sign of some sort that things were about to go right for him. It wasn't a matter of luck, but of natural justice. 'If I win the jackpot, do I get the money straight away?' He knew for certain that a fortune was waiting for him somewhere beneath the strips of foil. He should have had this money weeks ago. If he'd had money of his own, things would have been easier with Aaron. None of the trouble might have happened. With money, anything was possible. He could be in control. He could buy anything, anyone. If he chose, he could pay for the damage to the house and undo everything that had been done the night before. 'Only,' he thought, 'if he buys me a new fucking television. I'm not letting him get away with that.'

The man explained to him, patiently, the process for collecting a big win. The card would have to be verified, and taken to the post office, with two or three forms of identification, and a cheque would be issued.

'Can't I have cash?' He was on the eighth card by now. 'I need the money today.'

'I don't think so.' The man was looking at Nick warily. The conversation seemed to have gone beyond hypothesis.

'It's my money. I should be able to have it as soon as I like.'

The eleventh card was worth another ten pounds.

'Gimme ten more cards.'

'Are you sure?' The man glanced at the alarm button he'd installed beneath his counter, for reassurance. He had a feeling this one might end up nastily.

'Ten thousand would do. Is that too much to ask? I'm not even asking for the biggest prize.'

'Perhaps you should take them home with you,' the man said, indulgently. 'You'll need to have your identification before you can collect the money. You'll need to sit down and have a drink when you've won.'

The door opened behind him and another customer came into the shop. The counter was covered with used cards and foil dust. Nick decided to take the man's advice, for the sake of privacy, if nothing else.

The mess in the house was depressing. He saw the charred horse in the grate and it occurred to him that if he torched the whole house, all the evidence would be destroyed. Aaron would be poor and they would have to live on his winnings. It was a plan he could keep at the back of his mind. His options were open. Meanwhile there were the rest of the scratchcards. He opened the whisky bottle and took a drink from it. He didn't even like whisky, unless it was drowned in Coke, but it was a quick fix.

By the time all the cards had been used he was angry. He should have stayed in the shop. That was where the luck was. He'd never had luck in this house. He felt as though he had been robbed. There were ten thousand pounds somewhere that should have been his. If he had the money he would know what to do next. Now, he knew nothing. He didn't know whether everything was finished between him and

Aaron; whether he had somewhere to live any more. He had to talk to Aaron before he could know what to do next. He found the address book and called Susan, but there was only an answering machine. Then he realised that Aaron would have gone down to the country.

Mrs Gunn answered the phone.

'Is Aaron there?'

'Who is this?'

'It's Nick. Can I talk to him?'

'I'm sorry, no.'

'Please. I really need to talk to him. We had a bit of a row last night.'

'I gathered as much. I'm sorry, but he . . .' she was cut short by him interrupting.

'What's he been telling you?'

'Nothing, but I know my son.'

'Do you really? You don't know the half of it. What did he say? How did he twist things round this time? Did he tell you how he beat me up? Did he tell you I still have a black eye from last time?'

'I don't have to listen to this.'

'You fucking well do. There's a lot he hasn't told you. Did you know he used to fuck his ponies? I bet he kept that one quiet. I know everything, so you'd better let me talk to him.'

'You can't talk to him because he isn't here. He is in hospital.'

'What's the number of the hospital?'

'Don't you want to know what happened?'

'I know what happened. He drove off from here as drunk as a lord, after beating me up. That's what happened. He's lucky not to be in the nick. What's his number?'

'I won't give you that. I know my son.'

'No, you fucking don't. You don't know about Colm, do you? Ask Aaron how Colm died.'

'I'm going to hang up now.'

'Don't you fucking dare hang up on me.'

The line went dead, and Nick was as angry as if he had never vented it all the night before. He would, he decided, burn the house down. There was nothing to lose now. 'You bastard,' he kept saying, as though Aaron was in the room. 'You bastard. What would I do if you'd killed yourself? How dare you run out on me like that. You bastard.'

In the safety of the country, Mrs Gunn collected her son from hospital that afternoon. His injuries were not serious, the worst being a bad concussion, which was assumed to have been a result of the crash, even by Aaron, who had forgotten, for the moment, that he had been struck with a wooden horse. As a matter of course, he had been breathalysed, but there was no alcohol at all in his system. Nick had failed to notice that he had given it up, by way of example and encouragement, and was drinking ginger beer in the Twisted Arms the night before.

Aaron was a little weepy in the Landrover, and ashamed of it. He had not had cause to distress his mother by crying in her presence for more than twenty years.

'Are you all right?' she asked. She could sound quite tender at times, but that was usually while she was addressing horses. This was an exception.

'Sorry,' Aaron said. 'I can't seem to stop. It must be the shock.'

'Your friend phoned.'

'My friend?'

'The one who was supposed to be coming down with you.'

'Nick.'

'You don't have to talk about it,' she offered, 'now.'

'It's all right. There's nothing to talk about.'

She let him sob for a bit, and then said, in a matter of fact way, 'I have to say, he sounds a thoroughly unpleasant character.'

'He's all right,' Aaron said, 'really.'

'Really?'

'Really.' Having something positive to talk about seemed to clear Aaron's head a little. The tears stopped as inexplicably as they had begun. 'He's got some problems. We're working on them. He's alcoholic, I think.'

His mother made a noise, neither positive nor negative, but the sort of noise which encourages more to be said.

'Things aren't going too well at the moment, but he's such a nice man really, if you know him. He hasn't had much luck; a horrible life so far. I think I'm the first person who ever really loved him. Do you remember Bonfire?'

Another noise.

'That mare nearly went to the knacker's yard. But it was only because no one took the time to understand her. Do you remember I had her jumping gates by the end of the summer? No one is beyond redemption. Nick's just someone who's had a lot of bad luck. You should see him smile. It was the smile I fell in love with.'

They had reached the edge of the farm, and the first of three gates that had to be opened before the house. Whatever response his mother had in mind she chose to keep to herself, leaving his last remark to stand, unsheltered by concurrence or refutation.

'Are you up to opening the gates?' she asked. 'Or shall I?'

'No. I'll do it. I'm fine.'

He opened the Landrover door and put his foot to the ground. His leg gave way and he toppled into the grass verge. His mother came over to help him up, and he began to laugh. She laughed with him. It was

ridiculous: she, who barely came to his waist, supporting him.

'Sorry,' he said. 'You see, what a complete arse I am.'

'So you'll be going back,' she said, 'to him.'

They were both leaning on the unopened gate, she looking
at the scenery, because she could not look at her son. It being
her own scenery she was easily absorbed in it, focussing on
details without the need to take a general view. Since she
had first given birth all her nightmares had been about her
children. They were beyond her control now and she filled
her fears with the love of ungulates. She couldn't look at
Aaron because she knew there was nothing she could do to
help him. He had never been someone who could be told.
He had to find out for himself. In her pocket she fingered
a smattering of spilled oats, and in her mind she wanted to
ask her son what he would do, but she had heard enough
to know it was not worth asking.

'Will you be all right?' she asked, not certain of the context
in which she meant it.

'Of course,' he said. Beyond the curve in the road and the
dip in the valley, he could just make out the smoke from the
house. He had wanted, badly, to show this place to Nick, to
let him see that there was more to life. 'Of course,' he said.
'Have I ever been wrong?'